PROBLEMSKI HOTEL

PROBLEMSKI HOTEL

Dimitri Verhulst

Translated from the Dutch by
David Colmer

MARION BOYARS
LONDON • NEW YORK

Published in Great Britain and the United States in 2005 by
MARION BOYARS PUBLISHERS LTD
24 Lacy Road, London, SW15 1NL

www.marionboyars.co.uk

Distributed in Australia and New Zealand by Peribo Pty Ltd
58 Beaumont Road, Kuring-gai, NSW 2080

Printed in 2005
10 9 8 7 6 5 4 3 2 1

First published in Holland in 2003 by Contact Publishing as *Problemski Hotel*.

Copyright © Dimitri Verhulst 2003, 2005
Copyright © this translation David Colmer 2005

The publishers would like to thank, and acknowledge the financial
support of the Foundation for the Production and Translation of Dutch
Literature.

The publishers would also like to thank the Arts Council of
England for assistance with the translation of this book.

ISBN 0-7145-3110-3

Set in Sabon 11.5/14pt
Printed in England by Bookmarque Ltd

PART I

Bipul Masli, Photographer

Hargeisa, 1984

'Pretend I'm not even here!' I said to the starving child I was trying to photograph.

I was nervous and wished I had something to take to stop my hands from shaking. Somehow I felt that this would be *my* photo. *The* photo. The one that would signal the big breakthrough that would allow me to push up my market value, making it possible for me to ask the head honcho at Reuters if he could call back when it was a little more convenient. A photographer feels things like that. The world-famous Henri Cartier-Bresson felt it in Paris when he snapped that little boy with two wine bottles in the rue Mouffetard, Elliot Erwitt felt it when that black guy poked his tongue out at the camera, Alfred Stieglitz felt it when that beautiful girl with the even more beautiful fingers did her coat up at just the right moment, and, even after taking hundreds of photos of Greta Garbo,

Edward Steichen still felt it while getting his shot into focus: this will be it, the only true, beautiful, ultimate portrait of the goddess. The same thing I felt with that starving kid in my viewfinder. Bliss.

On nights that are no good for anything except bullshit, people sometimes claim that photography is mainly, if not totally, a question of luck. And then they all start off about the guy who took the one photo everyone knows: the naked girl, burnt, running with her arms spread – Christ with a cunt. Their line of reasoning goes that if the photographer hadn't coincidentally happened to be there when they were dropping the napalm, he could never have taken that photo, so therefore it's to do with luck. What can I say? You're not going to start grumbling that I had the luck to have a kid dying right before my eyes? I had the talent! Just like Robert Capa had the talent, the nose, to be there with his camera just where a soldier's brains were being blown out. Luck! According to mountaineers who have seen a murderous avalanche roar past a couple of inches in front of their noses, in the long run, luck is a question of skill. I know they're right.

The dying kid I wanted to photograph – I'd like to be honest about this – represented a dramatic and artistic turning point in my life. He converted me to colour photography.

As a student I was trained in the black and white tradition. A roll of colour film – at most that was something you'd buy for holiday snaps or wedding photos. Although there were some people who dared to add an arty touch to bridal shots by adding a splash of sepia now and then, usually with hilarious results. I have yet to see a wedding photo that was still worth its frame after the divorce. But that's by the by. The fact is, I always saw colour as trite. Much more than a colourist, I was a man for composition, someone who homes in on the composition in the things around us. LIGHT – *that* was important to me. In the Bible it doesn't say 'And there was colour.' It says 'And there was light.' Colour lives by the grace of light and that makes it inferior. As for the rest of it, I have to admit, that's all I've read of the Bible, but I think I've covered the most interesting bit. Anyway, I can't remember one person of my generation who graduated with colour photos. But there, in that hole, I definitely wanted to load a roll of colour in my Canon.

I almost never had any colour film in my camera bag, but that day I did. One roll. With twenty-four exposures. Twenty-four chances to make this skeleton-boy world famous. Twenty-four paths to the front pages of more or less all the newspapers they hand out on planes. I could already see the banner hanging out in front of all the major photography museums in this photogenic world: 'Bipul Masli Retrospective'.

The kid was in a magnificent setting: on a rubbish dump that he had crawled to with the last strength he had in him but where there was nothing even remotely edible left to find. For want of anything

11

better, he sucked on a finger and stared ahead helplessly. If I had used a polarization filter to cut the reflection on his eyes, you would have seen death deep inside. Something he had just vomited up was stuck to his stomach and stinking terribly in the heat. I gave him another three hours, four at the most. The angle of the light and the position of the sun would have been more interesting if he lived another five hours, but that was a risk I didn't dare to take. I wanted a portrait of him dying. Not dead – anyone can do that.

Animals and children are the most difficult to work with, just ask any of the great Hollywood directors. So I said, 'Pretend I'm not here!' and 'Just try to act natural!' Which was a very understandable request from my point of view. This kid had been mobbed by photographers, he'd seen more zoom lenses than rice dinners and looked at the birdie so often that Marilyn Monroe would have jumped at the chance to trade places with him. He'd already started getting used to the camera; if you didn't watch out he'd start posing, or grinning – it's possible, people are unpredictable. You see the same thing with all those glammed-up bimbos who make it onto the telly a couple of times in their life: they never get over it and even smile at the security cameras in department stores. But believe me, I'm not exaggerating when I say that this little guy must have been photographed at least a hundred times, mostly by freelancers who jumped on the first plane home afterwards to get back to their normal work: weddings, centenaries, car accidents… Of course, they've all got mortgages and kids to pay off – it's understandable. You could pave the equator with photographers, there's a lot of competition. But I don't work like that. Not at all. I wanted to take my time for a portrait.

It must have come as a relief to that kid, realizing that this was his very last photo session.

I'd done loads of portraits, mostly on commission to the weeklies that paid my rent at the start of my career. It's a shit of a job, take it from me. If you had to photograph a fashion designer, for instance, he'd have the presumption to think he knew best about which pose to take (blank look, surly mouth in Old Testament beard, bald head resting on hands in order to display the gaudy rings on all ten fingers), with pop starlets you'd have to keep begging them to keep their clothes on, and then there were writers. Writers are the worst. They go and live in dark houses so you have to drag all of the furniture outside to get a bit of light in the right place, and even then you still need a flash. You have to coax them in under the studio lights and then they sit there like an intellectual stiff trying to mime the word 'brainy'. Automatic release was invented especially for bloody writers.

I had experience galore with portraits, no doubt about it, and that wasn't why I was nervous. But the realization that I only had twenty-four chances to take *the* photo, when I'd usually shoot off fifteen rolls for a stupid mug shot in profile, *that* had me worried. It wouldn't be like that now with digital photography, but back then, in 1984, in the era that people sometimes wax melancholic about in today's dark rooms, we were subject to a lot more stress.

I smoked a cigarette, but it didn't calm me down. I was still shaking.

The tripod, then.

I begged the boy to stay alive for another half an hour. *Please*. It wasn't something I could make him understand, but it was in his own interest to co-operate. You see, I couldn't save him, it would be a bit naive to think otherwise. But in the West, this photo might end up on one of those calendars produced by peace-loving non-governmental organizations. That earns money, and that might be used to save others. His portrait could contribute to raising global awareness of the issue, blah blah. And, anyway, everyone dies of something. If it's not starvation, it could be salmonella chicken. His face, at least, had a chance of becoming an icon, and I, Bipul Masli, would be a manufacturer of the collective memory. Maybe they'd even turn him into a stamp.

I mean, did he think they were going to put *me* on calendars when *I* was dead?

Through my viewfinder it looked fabulous. A horizontal high-water line, indirect frontal light, yellowish sand that softened the shadows… Very, very nice… The boy was sitting in a sensual 'S' shape, you had a perfect view of those long, matchstick legs, the gigantic head, the swollen stomach spitting out its belly button... My finger was itching on the shutter release, but something was missing.

Flies!

World-wide there are some 12,000 different species of fly (*Muscidae*), which I won't list here, and at least half of those makes a living by tucking into camel shit or starving Africans. But truly, not a single species was represented on the head of that dehydrated child. Weird, everyone in those parts was constantly covered with flies, and even in my hotel room I'd cursed them often enough. The creatures cosy up together to drink from an eye like zebras at a water hole. But this kid didn't have any, and I felt like I was doing reality an injustice by not having a single fly in the picture. On the other hand, manipulating a photo clashed with my highly personal principles. And photos *are* manipulated. I know people who got included in the renowned World Press show with staged photos and made a stack of money off it. What should I do now? Could I call the hotel and ask them whether they'd be kind enough to quickly catch a fly for me to put on the kid's head, in the interest of a more representative picture?

I thought about it, it's true. For a moment, I *did* think about it. But by the time they got the fly in a jam jar and brought it here, my model would have been dead.

Click (x 24).

That same evening, when I pulled the photo out of the bath in my improvized dark room in Addis Ababa, it was immediately apparent: this is an almost perfect photo. Almost, because perfection would have been that fly.

Crapopia, 1974

I have sometimes dreamed of using this story in my standard opening speech for exhibitions and reaping success with it over and over again, and in my wildest fantasies the famous biographer Eric Nosensin starts the story of my life with the same anecdote. Namely, the account of how my career as a press photographer began when I was twelve years old, on my birthday to be exact.

Back then, Crapopia had not yet become the powder-keg it is today, the country was still in hands that didn't tremble. We lived in the capital, in a neighbourhood that could actually be seen as a cosy provincial home where children collected the ingredients of future daydreams on park benches. We didn't have much, but it was enough. There was a marching band and there were pubs where the band could stop. The first girls' bottoms we saw belonged to the majorettes, and the city's rugby team lost every week to oblige the canteen manager, who understood that fans need to drown their sorrows. Female teachers bottled up their hormones and grew moustaches, important meetings were held at the grocer's, the only voice you heard from the stage of the amateur theatrical society was the prompter's and brides were invariably pregnant...

Traditionally, a twelfth birthday was an excuse for the parents to get completely shit-faced, so my parents, who were great sticklers for tradition, made sure that by two o'clock we were sitting in our local, The Wet Afternoon, which was *the* gathering place for our whole neighbourhood. There, between the clicking of dominoes, you could always hear the heavy breathing of the licensee. His wife, fat Narcis, thought she could sing and did little else.

Before heading off to the booze-up, we had an extended lunch at home with the whole family. And when the serviettes were crumpled and dirty and the afternoon's first burps had sounded, it was time to give the birthday boy his present. A twelfth birthday was seen as the first step to adulthood: I stopped being a child when I got up that morning and pulled on my best suit which I would spill soup over later in the day. To emphasize this coming of age, it was customary to give something valuable on a twelfth birthday. Something durable that couldn't be associated with the world of a child. With girls there was a good chance they would get holes punched in their earlobes for their first gold earrings. Boys usually got a wristwatch or a bracelet with their name engraved on it. Stupid stuff really, useless enough for grown-ups to love, but because it made you feel like you had been accepted as a member of the segment of humanity that counted, you were happy to get it. It was also the day on which you were allowed to smoke your first stinking cigar, as long as you promised not to inhale. Once you had turned twelve, people like barbers called you 'Sir' – that had a certain appeal.

But I didn't get a watch or a bracelet.

My parents must have noticed me spending a lot of time in front of the photographer's in the previous few months. First, ogling the books on nude photography he had on display in his shop window. Later, looking at the cameras I dreamed of using myself as a nude photographer. I had an older and a younger sister. The older one already had hair on her thing, surely she wouldn't mind laying her homework aside for a moment to stand in front of my camera in the nuddy. For the sake of art, truly, not for my benefit at all. My father, virility-obsessed like all Crapopians, kept a collection of dirty books on his bedside table, but never before had I stopped to think that someone needed to photograph all that flesh before they could put it in the books. This made the prospect of having to go out and work one day much less gloomy, and my school results increased dramatically: the sooner I could start work, the better. When my father wasn't home, I hunched over his porn studiously, sketching poses that my oldest sister, and maybe her friends, could adopt for me. I even thought up a few variants of my own that I kept in a special folder that I reserved for that purpose and had labelled 'Maths' just to be on the safe side.

My parents gave my dreams a tremendous boost by giving me a camera for my twelfth birthday. I would have been even happier with a Yashica or a Leica, but the cheapest model Kodak was enough to make my day. And to get me off to a flying start, they had also included five rolls of film. Black and white. Now it all came down to how persuasive I could be with my oldest sister and her girlfriends.

I took the camera with me to The Wet Afternoon, there was no question of my ever going out without it again. Maybe I could score my first bull's eye, a shot of Dad when he was drunk and oblivious, for instance. Because there was one thing I was sure of, I wasn't destined for the messed-up snaps you find in almost all photo albums. I was soon proved right: my father hadn't even finished his first bottle there in The Wet Afternoon when the shooting started. It was the rebels – in those days they were still in their early phase. I don't know what possessed me, and it was all too confused to take my memory as a reliable source, but I don't think I lay down on the ground. I stayed standing and took a photo: of my oldest sister at the instant they fired the bullet went through her head. It wasn't what you'd call a conscious act. Try to see it as a photographer's instinct – I do.

It wasn't the photo I had planned to one day take of my oldest sister, and with a Canon the result would have been significantly better than it was now, with a trashy Kodak, but considering the circumstances it was the best possible photo that could have been taken in that place at that moment.

The film rewound automatically and people had already started crawling out from under the tables before things really got through to me. Fourteen people were dead and one of them was my oldest sister. A gunk-splattered man came up to me, introduced himself as a journalist, and asked whether I had really taken photos. 'Yes,' I said (or did I just nod?), and he asked me how much money I wanted for the film. I don't remember how much I asked, I don't even know whether my price was ridiculously low or unreasonably steep, but I got it. Immediately. The next day my photo was in the paper, on the front page. Photo: Bipul Masli. That's what it said. With the 'c' for copyright in front of it.

There, that's where my life as a press photographer began. With a substandard photo, underexposed and taken at too fast a shutter speed.

PART 2

Bipul Masli, Asylum Seeker

Somewhere Between Brutality and Britannia

This is no weather for hiding in a container. What must it be now? Minus five? Even colder? I haven't got a clue, but it's definitely freezing; the puddles have turned to glass and the Africans are going bananas. This morning, just before seven, they looked out through their window and saw that the sorry patch of grass under the clothesline had turned white. Of course, the grass is always greener on the other side, that's true here whether you're black, yellow, red or purple, but this morning those Africans couldn't give a stuff about that.

Snow! Block 2 (where most of the blacks are) was in uproar. The only place those guys get to see snow is on the Kilimanjaro. Given the lack of, among other things, snow in Africa, almost half of Block 2 sprinted out to scoop up that meteorological miracle.

The Chechens cracked up. A Chechen and a black – that is not a good combination. It really isn't. They face up like Maria Callas and Renata

Tebaldi on the same stage. If the two of them have to share a room, you can start ordering the coffin even before they've decided who gets the top bunk. And if you hear someone yodelling the soul out of his body, you can rest easy about betting a few cigarettes that it's a black being taken apart by a Chechen. They're all into kick-boxing, those guys, and it shows: a chest from here to there, and ailing kidneys from all those knees and kicks. You smell that when they've had a piss. You see it when they forget to flush. The colour of real ale. With maybe a splash of blood.

But like always and everywhere, you're better off not having any wild fantasies about what you might end up seeing in reality. Beautiful women. England. Snow. The Africans feel cheated, they had a different idea of snow. They thought you could grab it, make balls of it, throw it around... To the great hilarity of, again, the Chechens.

It wasn't snow out there this morning. It was frost. But how do you translate that? The Russians hawk a few sounds up from the back of their throats and scratch their brush cuts, but have no idea how to explain in sign language what frost is to an African, where it comes from, why it's not snow, who in God's name invented it and what the word for it could possibly be in their jungle dialect.

Frost. I wish it translated as *'poesia'* or something like that. But I can't bring myself to say it. Nobody would believe that *'poesia'* is going to turn up around here. Not out of the blue. And definitely not on that patch of grass under the clothesline. Goddammit, it's the same line that Sedi tried to hang himself on not so long ago. He failed, making himself look totally ridiculous in the eyes of some. But we're respectable people and don't mention the word suicide, at most we'd talk about 'putting an end to it'.

Anyway, Sedi almost put an end to it, something everyone around here thinks of doing at least a couple of times a day.

Sedi comes from Sierra Leone, a country the whole world feels sorry for, including the Aliens Department. Sierra Leoneans stand an excellent chance of a positive decision – everyone knows that, including Sedi. But after two 'negatives' he dropped his bundle. Now he walks around with a face that wouldn't be out of place on an aid organization calendar. Apparently an Amnesty International lawyer has got onto his case in the meantime and that doesn't happen to everyone, so he should stop whinging the whole time. You see, according to the recent rankings of the Human Development Report of the United Nations, this being a list of the countries where the living is easiest, Sierra Leone was right at the bottom. You've got to be in it to win it, and someone has to come last. You can use things like that to impress the officials in Brussels during your interview. I know people who would chop off their right arm to come from a country like that. 'Good afternoon, I come from the most pitiful country in the world and would like to apply for asylum.' The Chinese, for example, have risen to 96th with a bullet and that means a serious drop in their chances of getting a passport. That's why people think Sedi shouldn't carry on so much. His behaviour is very strange though. Most of the Africans around here walk around being cheerful the whole day long, with the exception of those moments when a Chechen is scrambling their insides. If you ask me, they need to do something about all that cheerfulness, otherwise there's no way the Ministry of the Interior is going to buy it, the idea that their life back there was significantly worse than the average camel's. Asia from Block 4, for instance, swings her ample posterior roguishly and sings while scrubbing the toilets. That arse and her singing...shit, man. We advise her to work on a gloomier mug if she wants those guys in Brussels to believe that her vagina has been shredded and that she's stormed Fortress Europe in the hope of saving her daughters from that same fate.

Trimming genitals is culture. Not trimming genitals is civilization. Human beings are culture-loving mammals.

Asia has already had two negative decisions, she's only got one life left and then they'll put her back on the plane. Travel broadens the mind.

In the old days they deported asylum seekers on the Belgian national carrier, Sabena. Sucker And Bimbo Express – Not Avoidable. Nowadays that airline is making a beeline for bankruptcy, which means that, in the near future, rejects might fly Lufthansa back to their mess of origin. The uniforms of the hostesses and the cabin service for our trip back can only get better, at least, according to Eizee, who's already on his third attempt to obtain asylum here and knows the Belgian travelogues they show as in-flight entertainment back to front.

The fact is, today is not the day to waffle on to any Africans about global warming. It's a completely insignificant problem and, to immediately declare the case closed, there's no sign of it happening anyway. Too cold to creep into a container. If it's true that the world is getting warmer from a bit of pollution, then it's high time to pour some extra chemicals into that nearby channel. Those factories down the road can't stink enough. It's freezing, it's frosting, and, unlike Chechens, Africans don't have the pleasure of having been created by some god or other with antifreeze in their blood. Even today, that gang from the Caucasus is walking around in short sleeves. Trying to stir things up. Having a little joke with Nicky the nigger. Just wait until *their* files get stuck on somebody's desk until next summer when it's like a pizza oven in the shade around here... We'll see if they're still able to flash those smiles when the blacks pull on their thickest jumpers just to tease them, when the jaunty Africans greet those sweat-drained polar bears with the words: I'm feeling just *dobre*... It'll be kick-box, *hombre!*

It's nine o'clock when the vestiary opens its doors. Vestiary is a word that has been chosen to sound as international as possible and does its best to mean something like clothes shop. On the cursed day that a group of moustachioed uniforms pull you out of that truck, in the sardonic hour that an X-ray detects your shivering body between a load of oranges and you end up here in the asylum centre, you don't get food rations, you get points. One thousand five hundred points, to be precise. To buy clothes with. An advantage of the point is that it is not subject to devaluation: 1,500 points is always worth 1,500 points. The vestiary itself is a room where the cast-offs of Belgian families hang neatly on racks and a polling booth does service as a fitting room. A woolly hat, to give an example, will cost you 25 points.

The house rules dictate that we are allowed to come to the vestiary just once a week, because otherwise we wouldn't do anything except try on clothes the whole day long in an attempt to dispel our boredom. That might be partly true for the women, but it's way off the mark for the men. Women are lucky in the sense that the ladies of Belgium are relatively fashion-conscious, fond of flaunting the latest model and more prone to throwing things out. Unlike Belgian men. They don't donate their socks to charity until there's five holes for each toe. But we don't complain. We're glad of a sieve to wrap our feet in. *Tank you, tank you berry much!*

The blacks discover that they might be able to stay in this country if they let themselves be turned into a coat or a pair of underpants. Skin from Africa seems to be doing well in the fashion world. But right now they're not particularly interested in leopard-skin knickers or any other African animal skins, a beanie's what they want. A thick one. And mittens. And a scarf. And I don't know what else. Nose-warmers? Do they exist? This weather is terrible. Especially for hiding in a container. With temperatures this low, you can only hope that no registered letters come tumbling into the letterbox.

No One Dresses Hair like Ramona Dresses Hair

He's always been scared of women, that's true, but the way the village hairdresser makes Rajib feel is in a different league altogether.

His hair has got so long it's started to curl up at the back of his neck and looks a bit like a hammock. Apparently your hair is still growing three weeks after your death, some cultures even take scissors into the grave with them. Consequently it shouldn't come as a surprize that even asylum seekers need to get their hair cut now and then. Even if Rajib does stare into the mirror sometimes, struck dumb that some kind of fuzzy growth is still putting down roots on his poor head. Call it hope – that things still grow on your body, even if just a bit of hair. He did manage to get rid of his pimples though, his mug is no longer a bloodbath every time he shaves. He needs every bit of fat he can get, his body lost all reason to push the pus out. He nourishes himself with little bits of pus.

When you're almost tripping over your own hairstyle, you can go to reception for a voucher that entitles you to a haircut at Ramona's Hairdressing Salon, some twenty minutes away from the asylum centre by rusty bike.

Ramona stinks. Rajib refuses to believe that it's perspiration. He's convinced that it's simply a matter of her having a body odour that's perfectly attuned to her appearance. She is fat without being voluptuous, her skin colour could justly be called fauvistic and, despite their untouchability, her breasts are menacingly horizontal. Her hair looks like she cut and blow-dried it herself. And although she's not his type, he can't stop himself from constantly thinking about her cunt, which is probably floating in its own juice in a pair of old-fashioned bloomers. Pickled cunt. It's something he's always suffered from: repulsive women terrify him and then he's overcome by the conviction that everything disgusting about them starts between their legs and swarms out from there, spreading all over their carcass. He used to feel the same way about his mother.

He puts his voucher down on the counter and smiles at her and at the ladies drying their hair in space capsules. He is scared of looking stupid. Ramona inspects the voucher that has been stamped by the asylum centre and looks him over from top to toe. She sniffs. In a flash he sees himself strangling the fat cow. He remembers the chickens he learnt to slaughter as a boy: Grandfather taught him to look at the bird's hole. When the chicken gives up the ghost, everything goes limp and white muck comes dribbling out. That's when you relax your stranglehold. He'd do it to Ramona the same way. She doesn't seem to like him much either. She points a severe finger at a chair, wordlessly, and he assumes that's where he's supposed to sit down. Between two stacks of magazines about effortless diets and celebrity geese. Next year's fashion in swimwear is promising. Boobs can get a bit bigger, blue will be the dominant colour and iron rods through belly buttons will be all the rage.

A dog, a Pekinese, hers or a customer's, has come over to rub itself up against his leg. It seems to have a thing about winkle-pickers.

Rajib feels the old bitches staring at him from under their curlers and behind their gossip magazines. They're talking about him and not for a second do they stop to think that he might understand their language, even if they do speak the dialect of a hole where the parish priest has consecrated inbreeding for centuries. They're talking about a foreigner, a dirty foreigner, the umpteenth asylum seeker, and for them the fact that the dog is furiously rubbing its pink crayon on his leg is incontrovertible proof that his family tree puts him with the quadrupeds. They guess at his origins and think up jobs for him: municipal shit-scraper, for example.

He knows the slut with the painted nails. Her face at least. She's married to the lawyer who founded the local branch of the Fascist Front. He lends his name to a party that's opposed to everything and in favour of nothing. If Rajib so much as touched his conjugal trollop she'd probably suffer an immediate aneurysm. Maybe he should stick his tongue in her mouth. That's what quadrupeds do, they slobber all over their owners' faces.

He can come and sit in the hairdresser's chair, says Ramona, and in order to treat him with the appropriate respect, she calls him by his surname.
Mr. Mokka.
'How would you like me to do your hair, Mr. Mokka? Frizzy? Rasta? Shall I shave it into a skullcap?'
The goats burst into a collective bleat, any minute now they'll start choking on their false teeth.
He could try to take his mind off things by counting their wrinkles, but right now he's preoccupied with other matters. Something to do with knives. And the canines of that little doggy.
He ignores the blatant way that Ramona reaches for the lice shampoo and smears it over his hair. A whole tube. It stings.
'This, Mr. Mokka, is what we call washing. Repeat after me: *washing!*'
'Why do Europeans wash hair that's going to be lying on the floor two minutes later?'
He closes his eyes and concentrates on Ramona's pudgy fingers as they rub the delousing product into his hair. As if his head is a ball of dough. Not that she does it gently. She's moved closer to his chair, her milk factories are resting on his shoulders and her tongue is dangling out of her

mouth as she concentrates on pressing those clumsy, stumpy fingers into his skull with all her might. She squeezes and pinches, and there's a good chance that soon she'll have his ears between the blades of her scissors. The water she uses to rinse his hair will be arctic, the hairspray will probably be an insecticide. Or one of those cans people use to cover the stench in a toilet. But he's enjoying it. He closes his eyes and lets his privates swell. If she'd just peek down at his crotch now – Ramona – and notice his hard-on. He can't help it and he's not sick. It's just been so long since anyone touched him in any way at all.

Cherribi Split

Where were you when they attacked New York?

In the long run, luck, according to mountain climbers who have survived a fifty-foot fall, is a question of skill. I don't know if they're right about that. Was it lack of skill that kept me from being in New York on that day, when I should have been there, with my camera, my Canon, to photograph those two shrinking white lines in that magnificent blue sky, giving that image to the collective memory forever? Was it because of a lack of skill that I, Bipul Masli, couldn't be in New York because my press card had been taken away from me by the dictatorship in my country?

No, instead of photographing the first iconic image of the new century, I was in Block 10 playing a fabulous game of chess with Cherribi, who's on the run from the Taliban. I thought I had everything under control, but he pushed a handful of pawns forward and sacrificed them brilliantly, blowing a hole in the middle of my position and forcing a draw. I don't mean it to sound as boastful as it does, but Cherribi has been the only person up till now who's able to silence me with a simple and therefore unpredictable move. Never before have I seen someone play so well with black.

After two 'negatives' Cherribi started getting nervous and three days ago he fled. To England. Despite having grown confident about the consideration of his file since September 11th. That day, the Afghans here took over the television remote control and nobody got it into their head to start blabbering on about whichever soap they happened to be missing. The Somalis, for example – they'd kill to watch a *National Geographic* documentary, probably hoping to catch a glimpse of the pets they left behind with tears in their eyes. But on that 11th of September we were all glued to the same channel. Cinema Inferno. Fantastic pictures, you have to admit. For a few hours after the fact, the Muslims were all shitting their tabinet pants, terrified of a vengeful massacre. But then newspaper article after newspaper article showed that the world finally seemed aware of the problems in Afghanistan, and Cherribi started to voice hopes of a 'positive'. Until the Americans dropped a few bombs on the place and began claiming that it would soon be straightened right out.

So it was two 'negatives' and repatriation was imminent. That really was something he didn't want to hang around for. There were a few of us in Block 4, where I sleep – Room 26 – who knew about his flight. Maqsood, from Kashmir, besides being my best friend here, was also Cherribi's mainstay, like a brother. He went to say goodbye to his brother, telling him that he'd had a tip about a container headed for England and that it was time for him to leave. They drank a glass of sickly-sweet tea together and then, probably for the last time, threw their arms around each other, hugging. And Cherribi split.

That's why you should keep your trap shut around Maqsood today. He's had another sleepless night, listening to the BBC news on his transistor radio non-stop from twilight to dawn. They intercepted a container with eight dead refugees. In Wexford, Ireland. The bodies are still nameless for the time being, but it's been established that they went on board in Zeebrugge. Where else? It's common knowledge around here, people know it all the way up the mountains of Kazakhstan, they talk about it in the cocaine stores of Tadzhikistan: the customs inspections at Zeebrugge are a joke, and the smugglers who demand a lifetime's wages to help us sing *The White Cliffs of Dover* know that nowhere is better for stowing away than those cheerless North Sea docks. But the bastards better make sure the container's not going to Ireland if you've paid for a trip to England. Ireland, that's the end of the world if you're shut up in a steel box, nobody can survive that. Especially not now. We told Cherribi – this is no weather for hiding in a container.

Maqsood is not taking it well. No one is taking it well.

We stand in the corridor by the radiator and smoke cigarettes. One after the other, if we could. But we have to make do with a single pack of baccy a week – the healthy side of being a refugee. We look down at the radio and take turns to rage at England. Not all of us are crazy enough to want to make the crossing. What do you want to go there for? The food's hardly any better than the fodder you get in the asylum centre. They lure in losers, you're welcome there without papers, all you have to do is sneak into a container and make sure you don't suffocate or freeze to death. It's like a children's game. Please Mr. Crocodile, May We Cross Your Golden River? Funny people, the Brits. By all accounts their sense of humour is as dry as dust, but still legendary. The best things they ever came up with are the Beatles and the BBC. The latter now states that there were five others in that particular container, they're hovering on the brink too, but at least they're alive. No names. But they're apparently Turkish, Albanian and Algerian, and the Irish Minister for Justice has promised to click his fingers and give them immediate refugee status.

Mussu's stomach is rumbling. He asks if anyone's got anything edible left in their room: a crust, an apple core... He's willing to pay fifty points for it, but there's nothing for him to chew on except his nails, if he's got any left. Maybe a few on his toes. It's his own fault – Mussu didn't touch his dinner tonight. Tomatoes, even if they didn't taste like it. Tomatoes with bread sandwiches. And tap water. Mussu can't bear the sight of another tomato, he coughs up bile at the mere thought. It's because he sat in the back of a truck full of tomatoes for two thousand miles. The people at the vegetable market must have jumped out of their skins unloading the crates. It was the strangest tomato they'd ever seen. So now everyone knows why Mussu also goes through life under the name of General Tomatski.

It's elbow work around ten o'clock when the newspapers arrive at the reception desk, we all want to know whether there's any news about our Cherribi. Those who speak a bit of Dutch grab *De Gazet Van Antwerpen*, the Africans lay claim to *Le Soir*. The world news is that Antwerp civil servants' lunch breaks are too long, that the English get so boozed up at Christmas that no one is able to go to work the next day – costing the state around 229 million pounds, that it's not the right moment to buy shares in a football team, that the Venezuelan president has upset his subjects by interrupting too many soaps for important messages, that the Chinese use Viagra to increase the potency of tigers and that someone has received an honorary degree for playing nice tunes on the mouth organ, but not that an Afghan has disappeared without trace after concealing himself in a container in Zeebrugge.

And then I suddenly hear a melody by Bach, which is nothing more or less than General Tomatski's GSM. We all have mobile phones, how else are we supposed to keep in touch with the mafia? We need to be able to arrange our containers when the Minister of the Interior gives us our marching orders.

It's Cherribi. He's alive. To reassure his old comrades, he's been nice enough to make a call. No problem, lads. Cherribi – just his style – made the mistake of stepping into the wrong container. He probably only half understood his smugglers and acted as if he knew exactly what they meant. Anyway, when he got out of his container (not tomatoes: butter and dope), he thought it was kind of warm for the time of year in England. He's in Spain.

'Hey, you slobs, how's it going up there? Not too cold? If they sell out of beanies in the vestiary, just come down here, eighteen degrees and a nice breeze.'

Maqsood knows his caliphs and today he'll mumble the right prayers to thank his Saviour. All our Afghani needs to do now is let himself get picked up by the *Guardia Civil* and in a few days' time he'll back in our Belgian 'home away from home'. Too bad for whoever's nabbed his toothbrush.

Naturalization Exercise No. 174BLZ18:
'Roger van de Velde Tells a Joke at the Pub'

Never before had Lode had a better chance to find out whether blacks really did have long penises and he was determined to take advantage of it.

He stood under the shower in the municipal sports complex washing the mud out of his hair. He went to football training twice a week; it was a sport he loved and he worshipped the group coitus of a goal. A pub team, nothing special. Recently his team had been reinforced by a black guy whose performance at practice already promised a lot for the game on Sunday. Fast and aggressive, fantastic ball control, a little showy perhaps in his attempts to create chances, but otherwise with an outstanding ability to read the game. Not a snide word was said about the arrival of a black player. What with marital worries and the vicissitudes of age, the team had whittled away so much that they could count themselves lucky to have eleven men at all.

Although it was something he thought about,

the question as to whether blacks really did have longer penises was not one of his obsessions. After all, there are more existential things to worry about. What was long, anyway? He'd even read somewhere that every penis was more or less the same length once erect and that any national or racial differences that may exist are only evident in the flaccid member. But still, now that his black team-mate was on the point of moving in under the showerhead, he couldn't resist the temptation to put an empirical end to the widespread doubt concerning the length of the black dick.

And yes, the difference was noticeable with the naked eye. Assuming that this man was representative of all blacks, Lode ascertained that the member of the black man *was* larger.

It slipped out before he knew it: 'But *why* do blacks have such a long one?'

The black, whose name was So – because they too have a mother who needs to call them in for dinner now and then – seemed to take this impulsive reaction in his stride and remarked almost in passing that it's possible for white men to have long penises as well.

A white guy with a big whang? How?

The black guy, So, explained the recipe for a foot and a half of masculinity, and that very night Lode was tying a brick to the end of his dick. It must have weighed at least two pounds, but it seemed in keeping with the laws of physics that any body part that was constantly subject to the tractive force of a brute weight could, in time, grow longer. There were, after all, cases of children with one long arm, namely the arm attached to the hand they used to carry their school bag.

The brick hung there like a sinker on a fishing line, Lode was determined to work, wash and sleep with it in place until the desired result had been achieved.

A week later, when So asked Lode about the progress in his underpants, he answered through a grin. 'It hasn't got any longer yet, but it's already turned black.'

Rocky

Just after asking me who I'm sharing with, people break into an embarrassed smile, both asylum seekers and staff. I don't think there's anyone who would be willing to swap roommates with me. It would be worth two packs of cigarettes to me, maybe more.

My roommate is Igor, a Ukrainian ex-pro boxer. The only reason people have for calling him Stravinsky is his first name, he doesn't radiate anything musical at all. Although perhaps he does have one minor similarity with the atonal composer: wanting to become French. Igor has set his hopes for a better life on the French Foreign Legion, he has a passionate longing to serve as tricolour-waving cannon fodder. Lately the pawns of the former red menace have received a warm welcome in the country that is famed for its cuisine, its kisses and its letters, but for the moment so many Russians have taken refuge in the Legion that they've imposed a temporary freeze. There's no room for Igor and they've chucked him on the waiting list. Meanwhile the hours tick away and his asylum application has almost been processed.

Igor will definitely be going on a journey in the near future, it's just the destination that's secret. It'll either be the jungles of Guyana for training as a master butcher, or he'll be on an accompanied flight back to the Ukraine. Or he'll take the last night container to England, that's another possibility.

Igor doesn't say much. Igor actually says nothing, *nada,* not a word. That's what scares me so much. Inside he's seething, the biggest fossil in the world could feel that, and sooner or later his fuses are going to blow. Look, I couldn't care less about his misery, I've got my hands full with my own misfortune, but I just hope he pours his heart out before he decides to take out his frustrations on my gob. Two taps on my trap and I'm dead. No doubt about it. Man, you should see his body, it's terrifying. And they're no implants. His ribs alone would be enough to feed the whole asylum centre for a week – that'd give us something to celebrate. His mug is a typical boxer's mug like the ones you see in glossy sports mags with drops of sweat being punched off their foreheads: a nose without a bit of cartilage left in it, number two haircut, flat forehead, eyebrows that have been sewn up about twenty times so that the skin over his eyes looks like a patchwork quilt. (A photographer's dream, Igor is, and if the smugglers hadn't been so mistrustful as to smash my camera, I would definitely have considered a portrait.) If Igor wants to shake my hand, I'd better hope there's a doctor in the house. Lately you could cut the tension with a knife and I don't dare to go to sleep until I'm sure he's in dreamland. I know it won't save me from a quick but very painful death, but I've still taken to keeping my cutlery under my pillow. You never know. But it's more likely that my fork will crumple on his chest. If you ask me, even bullets would bounce off his gigantic body.

Since he has such difficulty locating his mouth hole, no one in the block has any idea why he has applied for asylum. According to one person, Igor has an impressive police record in the Ukraine. Another says he's a deserter. A third claims he's on the run from the Russian mafia. Most important is that we know ourselves why we're here, that we have a good story ready for when we need it. And that we realize that we will never know just why they find it so easy to send us back to the monsters we're trying to escape. The Old Continent is full, they say, there's no room left for us. As if they always asked whether it was convenient before installing their colonies in somebody else's living room. But that's my personal opinion, and no one wants that.

When Igor talks to me – let's say that's about once a week and ten minutes max – he does it in French. That's for want of a better option, because his French somehow manages to be even worse than mine. A small, dark-green Russian-French, French-Russian dictionary helps bridge the linguistic gap.

The only one who succeeds in turning off the robot in Igor is Anna. A Russian. A fantastic piece of ass, who keeps her gorgeous body in an Adidas tracksuit. During her first hours in the barracks, I asked her if she spoke English. 'Yes,' she said, 'eh liddel bitch,' and she wasn't far wrong. If she gets three 'negatives', which is very likely, she will disappear from the records without trace. In high heels and with a fur coat covering her prime beef, she'll be off doing good turns for slobs with money to burn. How else is she supposed to make ends meet? And she's got the right trumps, so what's to stop her? To kill time and get in some practice, she sucks off Block 4 for ten cigarettes a pop. She smokes the first one as soon as she's gargled away the filthy taste.

Igor starts his day bent over his French books. It's far too fashionable a language for someone like him, but he still studies it with great dedication, three hours straight, without a break – his life depends on it. After practicing his vocab, he relaxes with a game of cards. Patience. Meanwhile it's gone twelve, and another half hour glides past while he chews on a sandwich. We make a game of trying to keep the food in our mouths for as long as possible, it gives us a sense of having something to do.

After lunch Igor reads the *MZ*, a Russian Sunday paper. The *MZ* is a dream of a newspaper, I'm jealous that there's nothing equivalent in my mother tongue. It has lots of photos (all ugly, but they're often the most interesting), ads for drinks that are so strong they'll make you forget the deepest misery, and puzzles that are so difficult that the new *MZ* will probably be down at reception before you've solved the puzzles in the old one. A chess column, a logic test with dominoes, a full-page crossword with inbuilt rebuses, palindromes, logogriphs and other linguistic acrobatics. Igor skips the joke section. And the last two pages are dedicated to naked female flesh. Hot bitches, tattooed sluts with room between their legs for thousands. After filling in enough words, Igor lies down on his bed and carefully studies the ceiling. He keeps it up until six o'clock.

In the evening he goes boxing. A club in a nearby hamlet has offered him free training facilities and, if they were going to put Igor in the ring with me, I wouldn't like to be a young boxer from that hamlet. The guy spends the whole day bottling up his rage, it must bloody well hurt when it comes out. No surprize, then, that he thinks the Belgian standard stinks – up till now they've only let him fight old ladies. But in the back of his mind he's keeping the option of finding the right papers here in boxing circles, star athletes just happen to find it easier to acquire a nationality. A refugee who wants to score in Belgium is better off being sporty than political.

When Igor comes back into the room, he stinks. His sweat is in a different category altogether, it reeks of fear.

His dinner has gone cold and he works the stuff into his mouth without any sign of emotion. I think it's supposed to be chicken. Chicken with bread sandwiches. And tap water.

And when he climbs up onto the top bunk, he takes the last two pages of the *MZ* with him. It doesn't matter to me. I like to hear the slats creaking above my head and I'm happy to have him wear himself out. Night after night, I wait until his newspaper stops rustling, his breathing settles down again, and he's sleeping soundly. Then and only then, do I dare to close my eyes and walk through my dreams with a camera. Colour film.

No Amount of Happiness Can Annul Human Sorrow

Every love story worth the name ends with a suicide, and that's something I can't put out of my mind when Lidia comes and slips her impressive five foot four inches in between my sheets. Her just coming into the room like that and snuggling up to me means, above all, that I forgot to lock the door, something paranoid Igor cannot stand at all. I don't even want to know how he would react if he knew that Lidia was lying beside me now, and who can guarantee that she, or the springs of this broken-down hospital bed, or yours truly isn't going to start producing sounds that penetrate the fathomless depths of his sleep?

I place a 'shhhh' finger of warning on the harps of her lips and she sticks it in her mouth. It's been a long time since I put part of my body in a moist cavity belonging to someone else and that makes me realize how lonely I am, making me feel even lonelier. If I could, I would cry. Then she lays a finger on my lips too. We'll be silent. Silent is what we'll be.

Lidia is what the ministry calls an 'AMA' – she's *alone*, she's a *minor* and she's an *asylum seeker* – it's a way to waste even less letters on her. She's already the fifteenth underage refugee to arrive in this building after undertaking the odyssey without friends or family. All our relations are distant and we're condemned to that distance for life, her as much as me, the younger and the older, but children who don't move with the herd grow old before their time.

Sometimes I notice a new sad face in the refectory, yet another person who's been fished out of the back of a truck, someone else who got their first impressions of this country in a service area on the motorway, and every day the sight of this massive influx of failures affects me less. And less. And less. Until it doesn't affect me at all. But I remember Lidia's arrival. I saw her arrive and I knew it was something I wouldn't forget – I felt that immediately. I was standing by the entrance gate, standing, smoking, trying to think of something to think about, something I wasn't too scared to think about, and looking out at the world beyond the barbed wire, which is not inviting, but which we dream of being allowed to join, and sooner rather than later. Nothing happened, nothing was what I expected and I felt no joy at the fulfilment of my expectation. Bad times go slower. I had been rolling a cigarette for fifteen rainy years and was waiting for the next meal to give me something to do. One of my teeth was loose and I was ecstatic at being able to play with the rotten ivory with my tongue. Then a police car drove onto the grounds and two uniforms led a girl into the offices. And time skipped a little.

Why did I think that she had a violin in her bags? If I hadn't thought she had a violin in her bags, would she have had a violin? Of course, I knew I spent hours a day on the lookout near the fence, foolishly hoping they'd toss in a refugee with some kind of musical instrument in their bags, even if just a mouth organ, a tin whistle, a bit of string from a smashed guitar... I was in need, desperate need, of music, not of the tapes that get played here ad infinitum and have the dubious quality of never breaking completely, just stretching and deforming the sound. But someone who has to cross a mountain ridge by foot just to catch sight of the next ridge and the following minefield, who has to squeeze body and possessions in between boxes of tomatoes, who has to hide between swine being taken to slaughter, covering themselves with a layer of pig shit at every border, someone like that leaves their violin at home. The only luxury worth taking as ballast is the Bible or the Koran, the last refuge in moments of desperation. And maybe a snap of the people you've left behind. Every memory is an extravagance. Unaccompanied female minors can count themselves lucky if *they* come through it in one piece, what do they care about a pair of shoes or a violin? No, I don't want to know about the filthy ways she paid off a squadron of customs officials at the borders, or whether she paid the bribes with her mouth at the level of an unzipped fly, because I know it already. I am familiar with that photogenic little scene.

I haven't exchanged a word with Lidia. I've had it with greeting newcomers, smiling and introducing myself. I'm done with asking everyone where they come from, what they are fleeing and how many murders preceded their decision. In the end we all try to outdo each other in misery. If A says that the soldiers in his country broke both his legs, B says that it was even worse in his country, the soldiers broke all three of his legs, and then you can abandon all hope, because how can you get asylum with two broken legs, if they refuse to give it to someone with three? And then the speculation starts. All we do in the corridors is smoke and speculate, that the European governments are into brain-draining, for instance, keeping the smart ones and stopping the broken legs at the gate. And there's no consolation in that either, because there's no reason anyone would ever would want to drain my brains, my brains are full of junk, full of muck, no government in the world would want the rubbish inside my head. And my head doesn't want that rubbish either. That's why I can't be bothered with newcomers and stand there getting caked onto the radiators with the others who have been begging for asylum for so long that they don't have the energy any more and despondently hold out their hands after their palms have been spat into two times. I look out with the rest of them, in collective nihilism, at the frozen mist on the windows, the ice flowers and the patches of frost, until the postman brings me a letter that will start with, 'Dear sir...' and end by summarizing a series of articles from some royal decree or other and excerpts from the seven psalms of the Geneva Convention. Thou shalt continue to clack thy jaws if thou hath hunger. Thou shalt not commit the sin of wanting to better thy life. Thou shalt not be so stupid as to think thou canst escape the bullet on which thy name is written. Thou shalt not measure the worthlessness of thine existence against the norms of the West. Thou shalt not tarnish the Old Continent. Thou shalt behave according to the universal rights of the mongrel dog. Thou shalt bugger-all.

I don't want to keep on raving on in the company of others that geography has given us a raw deal, that I'm sorry that I was born in the wrong place, I'm sorry my sister got in the way of somebody's bullet, I'm sorry. More than anything else, I want to leave the newcomers alone to believe in a future for at least a couple of weeks.

I'm lying. Actually, I don't want anything anymore. Most of all, I don't want to worry any muse-like apparitions, which is why I've only looked at Lidia up till now. At her legs as they carried her to the refectory. At her mouth while she was chewing her food. At the wet prints she left on the tiles when she walked barefoot back to her room from the showers. And now she's lying next to me. My fingers want to carefully check that it's true. I don't know if it's something she does often, going and lying down next to someone in the night.

She's lying here now, that's all that matters. I sniff at her body. I bury my nose in her armpit, as if I've caught a whiff of truffle. But she doesn't smell. No different to anyone else. Because we all smell the same, goddammit. We all wash with the same greasy soap we get in our basic package, with the same colour flannel, and we wash our hair with the same shampoo that smells of the same apples, and I'd bet money that they all grew on the same shampoo-apple tree. If smell was our only sense, no one in the asylum centre would be able to tell themselves from anyone else. And I push my nose even deeper, I want to hide it inside her, so I can dig it out again in the spring. As far as age goes, I could be the man who raped my youngest sister before murdering her with the slowness of a torturer, so that I was glad when the pistol smoke rose up out of her mouth, and I find it difficult not to think of that now. I have to smell, like she's smelling me now, dog and bitch. Stay. Stay lying next to me. Until we smell the rain that refused for years to fall on our cursed villages. Stay. Lie. Your whipped carcass against mine. So that they might become bodies after all. And we will be silent. Silent is what we'll be. But together. Stay.

Chess for Experts

Shaukat rages that he's going to kill the staff and blow up the centre. Three Chechens are so friendly as to lend a hand to restrain him. The veins in his forehead have swollen up until they're as thick as train rails, the Kosovar he cooled his rage on is bleeding like a sacrificial bull and General Tomatski just missed an uppercut. A 'crisis situation' is what they call it around here. The staff, who we adore, with the exception of that prick from the activity centre, have all been through a 'conflict management' course, but this is a different crock of shit. During that course they practised with actors. One actor shouted 'filthy wog' at the other and the prospective asylum workers solved the problem under the watchful eyes of a panel of examiners. During that course, the knives were made of plastic. They can be grateful that the Chechens got involved now, that the Chechens are so bored that they're glad to get mixed up in a fight. At last, something to do! Kick-box, *hombre!*

Shaukat is the loser of the day, no doubt of that. For I don't know how many thousands of miles, he put himself and his wife in the hands of shady people smugglers. They hid in cesspools, crept into pig-filled trucks, crossed mountains in worn-out shoes, slithered under electrified barbed wire, and finally saw their odyssey end in a motorway car park in the land of his dreams, where they stuffed him and his wife half-dead in an asylum centre. He got a bath, a bed and some bread (the BBB formula), and should be grateful. The story of his journey is hardly likely to impress anyone around here, that goes without saying.

Anyway, Shaukat's wife has disappeared. Gone. Vanished. Alone, tee-hee. She's pissed off on him. Asked the management on the sly to be transferred to another asylum centre, got her request granted and is finally rid of her bloke. It can happen. The little lady nags the ears off your head until you're willing to pack your bags and take your chances of a better future for you and your family. You risk your life and then, when you've reached your destination, the little lady takes the step that would have meant death by stoning in her land of origin: she does a runner. Goodness. All for one and nowhere at all: you lead your love down illicit border roads and end up having to fend and tend all by yourself in a foreign country.

Shaukat adheres to a creed that reduces the importance of women to that of a piece of shit that's not even steaming. We saw him thrash her more than once. He didn't pull any punches.

Marital brawling is daily fare here, that's normal and you don't even need to be stuck in an asylum centre, but I've never seen anyone beat his beloved like Shaukat. Last month, for instance, he broke her wrist for joining a computer course. Women shouldn't go in for further education, they should stay backward – after all, backwardness is their nature. And so, in front of everyone, he broke the good woman's bones with a superb *waza-ari*. Shaukat never could count on much applause, but everyone has their own cross to bear, and we don't get mixed up in each other's affairs. When she was menstruating, Shaukat demanded another room and preferred sleeping outside in the freezing cold to sharing a bunk with an unclean beast. Only natural that we now delight in pointing out that, for a cow, his wife turned out to be pretty smart after all. She got her transfer and, by God, she's now in the asylum centre on the coast. That's even funnier. They've got a swimming pool there, they get private rooms and everyone has a TV of their own. She can sit back and watch porn movies if she likes, just as an example. She can swim laps in the pool every day, in formation with handsome men, training for the Channel. Just imagine the commotion when Shaukat gets a 'negative' and she gets a 'positive'! That'll be a day to watch the papers!

I don't know how they calmed him down again, maybe they stabbed him in the arse with a needle full of morphine, but by lunchtime the maniac was resting his head. Never would he forgive the staff for helping his wife with her divorce.

It doesn't have a thing to do with his religion, but nobody ever liked Shaukat and now that he's been taken down a notch or five, the atmosphere is festive. Bring on the streamers and the party hats. He's no better than a soggy newspaper the way he drags himself from one minute to the next. He even seems to have regret, remorse and repentance at his disposal. Put him in a habit and stand him on a pillar, he can fill in as a martyr. Just cover his doodle with a bath towel, and I'd immediately see St. Sebastian before me, with his mouth twisted as if he can't decide whether to cry or come, the arrow shafts still trembling in his side. Someone should advise him to apply for a job at the Vatican as the Biblical masochist in a *tableau vivant*.

I don't know what possesses me, but I'm sick to death of Shaukat's blubbermush and challenge him to a game of chess. Even a pig is human and it would be better for him to get his mind off things for a while. Since he insists, the stakes are five cigarettes.

If I felt like it, I could wheedle his five cigarettes off him in fifteen moves. He's already in trouble after I've moved my two knights into position according to the laws of a very classic opening. More or less all of his pieces are undefended. I have to be honest about it, I just can't bear it that Shaukat claims to be a political refugee. Okay, it's quite plausible that he is, that the politics in his country are completely fucked, and when he goes back the government will squash his head or stick his tongue in a wine press. Nowhere's perfect. But it doesn't show in the way he plays chess. He plays with the pawns and the king doesn't lift a finger. The king sits back with his courtiers and leaves all the work to the others, letting his subjects get wiped off the board to his greater honour and glory. And he keeps the queen, a woman, on a short leash. But I think, 'Let's take it easy today, the poor guy's lost his wife, we shouldn't trample him down even further,' and I give him no less than three chances to take my best piece. And, as if that's not enough, to help him back on his feet, I give him ten shots at an open goal, he can checkmate me just like that. But no, Shaukat's so thick he couldn't tell the difference between a turd and a shit and just bumbles on.

Five cigarettes, and I know that he's only got four left for the week. Being able to smoke must do you a power of good so soon after a divorce, wouldn't you say?

Fine, it's dragged on long enough, I do what I could have done an hour ago and move my bishop from b2 to f6. 'Checkmate, Shaukat!'

First he has to study the whole board incredulously. His nostrils flap. His upper lip trembles, revealing a rotten tooth. I'm starting to regret getting the arsehole out of his room, he doesn't deserve my friendship. Because, you see, now he does exactly what I expected, hurling the chessboard across the recreation room. All the pieces, the entire cavalry, go flying through the air as if the chessboard has been hit by a scud. Now I have to listen to him saying I cheated and swapped pieces when he wasn't looking.

I don't get my cigarettes.

And that, buddy, is something I don't take kindly. A promise is a promise. I want to hurt him, that's all he deserves, but I don't know if I have the nerve. I look around and see three Chechens standing by. I've got the nerve. No, I haven't. Yes, I have. I say, 'By the way, Shaukat, just last week, I gave it to your wife from behind.'

Rocky II

There's post for Igor. Registered. Covered with stamps and seals, the letter is lying in the middle of the table on top of the most interesting bit of photo in his Sunday paper. We know who wrote the letter, it's the only letter we wait for, but now that he's received it, after months of boredom, he's almost too scared to open it. Later. He wants to go and eat first. That's very sensible of him. The food is tasteless anyway, trying to stomach it on top of bad news would be too much.

It's bread sandwiches for a change. And coffee that tastes as if they've run the water through the same filter ten times in a row. If you ask me there's not even any caffeine in it – that would get us too excited. I have my own reasons for believing that they even mix bromide into our slops – it inhibits rutting. Nowadays I wake up limp, there has to be a reason for that. It's definitely not mental.

Of course word gets round that Igor has a letter,

and it does everyone wonders to find out that they haven't forgotten the address of the asylum centre down there in Brussels. Some people have been stationed here for so long, eighteen months or more, that they've started thinking their file fell into a waste-paper basket by mistake and got shredded. Speed is apparently not one of Belgium's strong points – that's good for if we ever find work here. People keep pounding on our door, hungry for news. And? And? But Igor leaves his letter untouched.

It's not until late in the afternoon, after hours more of studying the ceiling (which unfortunately doesn't have a single crack in it – that would have made for a little variation), that he grabs his knife in one smooth, fleeting movement and cuts open the envelope. He must have been thinking of a person the way he slipped that knife in under the flap. I saw it. I smelt it. His sweat betrays him everywhere.

And he sits there. With his letter. His fate. And he doesn't understand it. The bastards have formulated his future in Dutch. With a bit of luck you get fifteen minutes down there in Brussels to explain why you were flogged in your home country, why they burnt your house down and raped your daughters, why you were visited by an uninvited mob of robbers who thrashed your mother before your eyes and fed your father's liver to the dogs...and after months of twiddling your thumbs, tying your toes in knots out of boredom, you get a letter. One sheet of paper. More signature than text.

The letterhead says things you already know. No interpreter was present during the interview. There was no third person, no lawyer. They value the reader. Not much, but they do value him.

Dear...
On the basis of elements drawn from your file, I hereby confirm the decision of the deputy of the Minister of the Interior refusing permission to remain in Belgian territory. Referring to Article 52 of the Aliens Law I conclude that your request for asylum bears no relation to the criteria of the International Treaty concerning the status of refugees or to other criteria which warrant the granting of asylum.

Furthermore, I believe that in the current circumstances you may be accompanied to the border of the country from which you fled, and where, according to your declaration, your life, your physical integrity or your liberty were endangered.

Subject to another decision by the Minister of the Interior or his deputy, you are required to leave Belgian territory within five days of the date of notification of this decision. (Royal Decree of 19th May 1993: article 17, sect. 2, par. 2).

Lucky for him, Belgian legislation is as logical as Belgium itself: he has to leave the country within five days, but has been given thirty days to lodge an appeal.

These letters are boldly headed 'Confirmation Decision to Refuse Residence' and have therefore been formulated in language that passes itself off as Dutch. The language we can study here despite not having any certainty that it will ever become our means of communication. The language we obsessively study here as a means of killing time.

Outside, the thermometer reads minus six, and, although it's no weather for it, the BBC shamelessly interrupts a concert pianist to announce that another container of refugees has been intercepted. In Tivoli, Italy. This time it's supposed to be Rumanians. No tomatoes, they were hiding behind pallets of tiles. But we don't have to worry about having to share our rooms with Rumanians: they froze to death on their way from Nothing to Nowhere. A rock-'n'-roll death, on the road. Apparently it's not too bad, exposure – mountaineers who got caught in a blizzard on the roof of the world, and could count how close they were to the tunnel of death on their blue fingers, declared afterwards that they felt stoned out of their skulls while waiting for the helicopter.

Every conversation around here needs a cartload of dictionaries. This one too. Step by step, Igor and I unravel the secret code of the ministerial epistle, noting scraps of wonky sentences on a piece of toilet paper.

And when we discover the verb *quitter*, a much too regular verb, Igor sits down diligently at the table to prove his ability: *je quitte, tu quittes, il quitte, nous quittons, vous quittez, ils quittent.* The significance of this black-and-blue-stamped letter just doesn't seem to have got through to him. Maybe he hasn't done the immediate future in French yet.

Malcontents' Almanac

T.S. Eliot was wrong. Not April, but December is the cruellest month.

It's no weather to hide in a container, all the destitute desperados who try to ship themselves end up freezing to death between a load of tomatoes or tiles. The blacks have lost all of their elegance because of these temperatures, it's impossible to even imagine them walking down the street with a ghetto blaster on their shoulder.

The federal police could turn up any moment to seize my roommate like some gangster. For now he doesn't show it, he's lying in bed and waiting. But his blood must be boiling and I expect that sooner or later he's going to beat me to a pulp just for fun, out of revenge, to blow off steam, for no good reason.

Besides, we're knackered. For more than a week now, there's been a racket in the corridor every night. You're either being kept awake by a domestic argument, or else it's Anna needing a smoke and loudly squeezing juices out of men. Or little brats howling because their mother's undernourished or over-stressed and doesn't have any night-feeds left splashing around in her tits.

I want to sleep, damn it. A trillion years non-stop, but for now I'd quite happily settle for five or six hours.

And even if there's no fucking or fighting or crying or whining or complaining in our corridor, you can still forget about getting a decent night's sleep this month. All the Muslims, and they're definitely the majority around here, have gone to the computer class and checked out the Ramadan calendar for the year 1422 on *www.mbs.maghreb.com*. That is the year in which we are now living: the year in which they torpedoed the States with two high-flying *shahids,* whereas at that same point on their timeline, the Old Continentals hadn't even wiped out their first Indian tribe. The Ramadan calendar shows the official times at which Muslims are allowed to eat. In order to observe their religious diet with a minimum of discomfort, the Islamites have taken to living at night. Their cassette recorders are playing something that might be the *muezzin,* but could just as well be Arab pop music. I don't know the first thing about it and in the daytime I can appreciate some of those nasal songs and melodies. More than that: in an asylum centre there is nothing more beautiful than their music. Except Lidia. But their Mecca rock doesn't have to be turned up to volume fifty. And definitely not at three in the morning.

We find it astonishingly easy to respect each other's gods and she-devils, everyone has the right to fall back on the nonsense of their own choosing, as long as they don't bother other people with it or keep them up at night. But when your children start turning into brats because they can't sleep, tolerance becomes a difficult concept. Up till now the non-Muslims have dutifully put up with shit over or next to the toilet bowl. We understand that their Law obliges them to squat with their feet up on the toilet seat while squeezing out turds. But recently you hear more people cursing Allah while relieving themselves. The loo is no longer the place to relax and read the paper, and even General Tomatski has stopped retreating to the sanctuary of the smallest room for a wank. He no longer finds the atmosphere inspiring.

The food too has become an audible source of annoyance. Not a prophet in the world can help it that we don't get enough to shove down our throats, you can't hold any of the gods responsible for the fact that with a blindfold on it's impossible to identify the odourless substance on your plate. But to placate the feelings of the common denominator, we only eat meat that has been slaughtered ritually. This is not a hotel and anyone who wanted to line up for a smorgasbord should have made sure they were born in a country that respects human rights. Eat what's going, the same as everyone else.

I don't have a clue what the ritual of the slaughter might be, but if I imagine a chicken lying there with its blood gushing out while three butchers dance a raindance around its twitching body and a boys' choir (in trance) see the fowl off with a performance of the chicken requiem, then I remember what it's like to laugh.

Truly, the end of Ramadan can't come fast enough, because with the mood the way it is at the moment, the smallest frustration is too much and will be taken out on a Mohammedan. And I'm on the cleaning roster this week. I may be famous in Block 4 for my willingness to work, 'The Man Who's Happy When He's Finally Given A Chore So That At Last He Can Better His Boredom,' but scraping intestines off the wall just isn't my thing. I'd rather be bored. May they start living in the daytime again as soon as possible, let their *Id al-Fitr* arrive quickly so that they can celebrate their Sugar Festival with five sachets of sugar in their coffee. You have to make do with what's available.

That Islamic celebration is just one in a long line and that's what makes December so gloomy. It gives you a sense of festivity.

Recently they had Saint Nicholas. That's a guy with a cotton-wool beard and a *lorgnette* without lenses. He gives our children teddy bears that have spent years in the arms of Belgian kiddies who have worn them out so much that they can now belong to us. The servant of the aforementioned cotton-wool-beard-wearer is black. This place is full of blacks, but they still got a whitey from the village and smothered him with shoe polish. The black's job is to scare our children. If the children have been naughty, the Moor stuffs them into a sack. These Europeans have strange holidays.

Soon the Christians will celebrate Christmas. They have a tree, which they decorate with tinsel boas and fragile balls. It's also hung with lights that get on your nerves. In the village, melancholy jingle-jangle music blasts out of the PA system and the prices in the shops have skyrocketed. At the market there's a stall with a sheep that stands there bleating and wondering what it's doing between all those plaster statues.

Then comes New Year. On New Year's Eve the town council is going to shoot so much worth of fireworks up into the sky that we'd rather not see any exploding balls of fire at all and have an extra plate of food a day instead.

Then comes the Orthodox New Year.

Then three fools dressed as Gypsy kings sing that they don't have any money to flush down the toilet. *Nahnou moulouk el shark al thalatha.* We are three Kings from the East.

Then it's New Year for the Chinese.

It's a party, it's a party, kiss my balls if we've ever had this much fun here before.

Not April, but December is the cruellest month. In December the prophet of the Old Continentals saw the light of day. In April he died.

Insomniacs Have Conversations Sleepers Would Never Suspect

If Igor Stravinsky murders me, which could happen any moment now, I hope he does it fast. A smashing blow on the nose so I lose consciousness and collapse on the ugly tiled floor and don't need to scream while he guts me with his pocket knife. The worst thing about it is that I can forgive him for it already. I'll know he's not out to get me in particular, I'm too insignificant for that. I'm just the guy who drew the short straw and got to share a room with him, thus becoming the first person in reach when he decides that the time is ripe for retribution. I can't deny it, when I was a kid I occasionally booted a faithful dog in the snout because my father had, for didactic reasons, given me a whack on the back of the head. And that all turned out fine. Nowadays I'm the biggest animal-lover around.

Secondly I hope that once you're dead you're dead. Please don't subject me to some kind of unexpected hereafter where I have to start off by applying for asylum. If God used his perpetual playground as the model for this planet, you can bet your life that the beyond is one big bureaucratic mess. How many forms will I have to fill in, how many stamps will I have to obtain once I get there, and how many committees will have to spill their coffee on my file before I'm allocated a tiny room that I have to share with an angel that only speaks Russian? I mean, I've had that already, it was wonderful. Thanks, but no thanks, I'll see you later.

It is a reassuring feeling though, already knowing your murderer, that's an advantage, one less uncertainty, but that doesn't mean I'm ready for it.

I dread the night. I dread every night and I'm tired of staring up at the bottom of Igor's mattress with wide-open eyes until I'm sure he's dropped off. And he's not going to drop off in a hurry because our block is a disco again, the Kosovar toddler next door is crying from hunger. You'd have to do about thirty thousand push-ups to exhaust yourself into snoozing in these conditions. I never push myself up, for the simple reason that I think it looks stupid, and so I go and knock on Maqsood's door, knowing that you can find him awake at any time of the day or night.

He has saved enough tea for numerous, yet to be acquired, friendships, and lowers two bags into the lukewarm tub of water he used to wash his feet this evening. We don't complain.

Maybe he feels like a game of cards? I can put up seven cigarettes.

Yes, now that I happen to mention it, he wouldn't mind playing. He knows a fun game, something Pakistani.

Maqsood speaks enough English for a pop song, maybe it will also be enough to run an all-night supermarket here later, or to skip from bar to bar selling roses to paralytic sweethearts. They're not unreasonable options for a future. But explaining a card game is beyond him.

He deals. The cards he popped into his backpack one day and smuggled along with himself across no less than twenty borders are decorated with female nudes. Even though neither of us has the slightest clue what game we're playing, Maqsood deals the women and tells me I have to lead.

I play a card. Four of hearts. A redhead with a snake around her neck.

He covers it with a hot bitch in an acrobatic pose, ten of spades.

I throw down a jack of diamonds (the kind of Chinese takeaway they sell at European matrimonial agencies) and scoop up the cards. No reaction.

But then, after a long pause, he says 'congratulations', probably because he feels that I'm waiting for a comment. If only I knew why my action was congratulatable. I'm just doing the first thing that comes into my head, like a little boy who holds a fan of beer mats in his hand and thinks he's playing poker.

It goes on like this the whole time until the

game's dead simple rule, and there is only one, gets through to me: whoever has enough energy to pick up the cards that have been played wins the trick. It comes down to just one thing: trying to be the least apathetic of the players. An excellent game for infant schools, psychiatric institutions, drug rehabilitation centres and refugee asylums.

In the corner of the room Das, Maqsood's roommate and ex-Tamil Tiger, is reeling off Catholic prayers. You never know, it could help. Das's village was probably once visited by the missionaries of the *Congregatio Ejaculati Cordis Mariae*. They built huts and schools, fucked natives and converted children to the one true religion. I'm sick to death of his bullshit chanting and if he keeps on thanking the Lord for the beauties of life, I'm going to go over there and give him a kick up the arse. I don't mind anyone telephoning God, especially not at night rates, it's up to them. But please, do it quietly. I get embarrassed listening in to the intimate conversations of strangers. When I notice that Maqsood has started weeping in the meantime, I really do start to feel sorry about having come to visit. Igor has probably dozed off by now with the MZ beside him. What am I doing hanging around in this room?

And Maqsood, in turn, is sorry to be bothering me with his tears. He is genuinely sorry. He drops to his knees to soak another teabag in the tepid washing water.

'Don't be daft, it's not a problem! If you sat here

giggling, that would really confuse me.' How else am I supposed to react to Maqsood's melodrama?

He shows me a box of sleeping tablets with a very poetic brand name. Prescription drugs always have beautiful names. The more fatal, the more beautiful. He can only get to sleep now after scoffing down half a box. It's not even a question of being able to sleep, but of wanting to sleep, of daring to sleep. Sometimes he wakes up drenched in sweat, screaming, shaking like a leaf. Then he's back in Kashmir. In a cell. For voting for the JKLF.

Maqsood doesn't have any white left in his eyes. His eyeballs are red and the colouring technique was invented by the prison wardens of his home country: lock someone up for fifteen days in a dark cell that's no bigger than the lift in a cheap suburban apartment building and fit it with a vaporizer that releases pepper spray as constantly as the smell of pine forest is wafted through your average toilet. All his dreams last fifteen days.

And the setting of his nightmares goes beyond the cell. In front of his red eyes he sees them killing his father again, bit by bit, so that it hurts. Skilfully enough to make sure he doesn't lose consciousness. He sees the same thing happening to his children. And again he sees his wife tied up on the kitchen table while a cordon of policemen and local councillors argue amongst themselves about who gets to screw her first. Again he sees the leader of the gang walk out as proud as a peacock with her clitoris between his teeth.

'Just touch my button!'

Dips and bumps, a paradise for little boys

looking for adventurous terrain for their toy cars, a dream for photographers hoping to impress the editors of *Magnum*.

'It's from the rifle butts. My stomach looks like an embroidery pattern since the doctor dug the bullets out.'

Silence falls. I don't dare to think anymore. Das has stopped thanking God and I have absolutely no idea what to say. I mean, I've suffered my share of obscenities too, but my gut hasn't been torn open and up till now I've only been smashed in the face with fists. Otherwise I could have taken off my shirt and cheerfully compared my bullet scars to Maqsood's. What do you do in the depths of a miserable night? I'm determined to understand why Maqsood has something against all those refugees from the Eastern bloc. In his view, they have no right to this odyssey. They feel justified in packing their bags and seeing their lives as poverty-stricken because they live in a hole that doesn't have a branch of a hamburger chain. 'Economic refugee' is a term of abuse here, because improving the quality of your life with two dried-out sandwiches a day is not recognized as a universal human right. The Geneva Convention has spoken: you can die from poverty, but not from bullets. Because the latter shames democracy.

'I think I'd better hit the sack.' The wording makes me sound pretty much like a shit, but I can't think of a better way to put it. Maqsood gathers up the cards and puts them back in the box.

'You owe me seven cigarettes,' he says, 'you lost.' And as is usual with a great loss, no one knows exactly why.

Our Sad Children Are the Future

The Prosineckis' little boy came home from school today with a beaming smile. He was grinning ear to ear and it's a shame he lost part of his face in a bombing raid because otherwise he would have been a beautiful child for as long as that smile lasted. 'Stipe' is the little rascal's name, he's as old as his sorrow, and if I'm ever unlucky enough to have a son myself, it would be a consolation if he turned out like Stipe. Preferably, of course, in a version with a whole face.

Stipe's got talent, even if being born in hell increases your chances in that department, and that's something I'm quite willing to believe. Talent is a dungflower. But still. He's not the only kid here who, encouraged by the child psychologist, spends his evenings in the activity room taking on his brief past with a box of coloured pencils. They all draw the same gory scenes with bombs and knives and machetes – the predictable themes. As far as that goes, Stipe's no different from the rest of them. He too reaches for the red pencil more easily than, say, the green. The wounds he draws, or rather, *carves* into the paper with his needle-sharp pencil are no more expressionistic than the little masterpieces the other kids his age draw, but I always find his composition slightly more intelligent. The lad has a feel for perspective too. For someone his age he's a good chess player, he's not bad at table tennis and he's an enthusiastic singer, even if he can't hold a tune. And when he sings, he always misses the right notes. Actually, I'd rather he didn't sing. Little brats who play the choirboy always make me cry – I'm a sucker for artistic platitudes. Maybe later he'll be able to afford an extra tin of dog food a day by playing tearjerkers on a fiddle in the high street: a busker with a stuffed-up face can still do quite well. Anyway, I like him, and it did me good to see him coming home from school with his mouth forming a broad bridge between the perfect half of his face and the caved-in half.

School attendance is compulsory for our children here in Belgium and as a result they're more streetwise than their seniors and quicker to learn dirty words in Dutch. Stipe's latest linguistic acquisition is 'fuck you' and he's proud to see his vocabulary growing. Every weekday the children are dragged out of bed half an hour earlier than the adults so they can get their schoolbags ready before a social worker arrives to cart them off to the local council schools on public transport. Because of the dispersal policy they all go to different schools. Like everything else, this is for our own good. The reasoning is that if the children from the asylum centre were all in the same class, they wouldn't be so keen to integrate. It's probably true.

Which leaves Stipe sitting somewhere at the back of the class chewing the end of a biro. Unless his classmates take the trouble to use simple words and speak very slowly in Standard Dutch, he doesn't understand them. He doesn't understand them. Playground football is the only language they have in common and the one thing he's picked up from his education here is that Belgians can't shoot. Stipe has a more graphic take on it: he claims that Belgians kick the ball as if it's a person. I told you he has talent.

But he can't read or write. The lessons go too fast for him and he really has nothing better to do than sink his teeth into his pen and pass the time until the bell rings gazing at his teacher. It's too bad for Stipe, but if I was him I would have demanded another teacher if she's only there to be stared at the whole day long. Mr. Prosinecki recently asked me to go to the school with him for some kind of parent-teacher evening, and I got a look at her. If Stipe used his crayons the way she uses her lipstick, he'd fail art. If you ask me, her hobby is knitting in front of the telly. During this famous parents' evening she didn't have much to say about Stipe. What did *she* know, after all? The boy sat there in the last row under the map of coveted Europe, sucking his pen and staring at her. Drawing, he was good at that. And gym as well. ('It's a shame the Eastern bloc has been abolished, Mr. Prosinecki, otherwise I'm sure we would have seen your son shine at the Olympics. I love that, gymnastics. Especially the exercises on the horse.') He always got an F for reading and writing, but could just manage the sums. She was sorry she couldn't spend more time on him, but, well, we had to realize – '...you see, you know, you understand, don't you, Mr. Prosinecki?' – there was no point in teaching the boy to conjugate verbs when it was quite possible, just to pluck a figure out of the air, that three weeks from now he'd be kicked out of the country and never hear a word of Dutch again. She had another thirty-four children in her class and although some of them might not have the intellectual capacities of a guppy, there was at least some point in pounding certain information into those tiny little heads of theirs.

We saw, we knew, we understood.

Stipe can really drag his feet after another day at school. Sometimes when I go to pick him up from the bus stop he gives the impression of being about to collapse under the weight of his own superfluousness. But not today. He was smiling. And that came as a relief because it was his birthday, his sorrow had just turned ten. He's all his fingers old.

The displacement of air during the bombing attack in his drawings sucked the right eye out of his skull. Apparently that's not too bad when it happens, the pain comes later. Stipe has, or had, brown eyes, but the only glass eyes in stock were blue. Although possibly fashionable, something like that does tend to spoil the appetite of table companions and makes dawdling in front of the mirror fairly uninviting. This morning at breakfast, the management of the asylum centre presented him with a brown replacement eye. It doesn't always have to be a comic book or a teddy bear. Stipe couldn't have been happier and things only got better. At school his class had made it into in the final of the football competition and *he* scored the winning goal. The other boys carried him round on their shoulders. And after that, he celebrated a traditional Belgian birthday. I'm not that familiar with Belgian traditions, but Stipe told me about it: everyone gets to write a birthday wish on your body with a thick greasy felt-tip. Once they've all written their wishes on you, they stand around in a circle and applaud. He had wishes all over his stomach and all over his back, did I want to see them?

Stipe pulled up his jumper proudly and I read, 'Go back to your own country, dirty wog.'

'Well? Well? What's it say?' he asked. 'Can you translate it for me?'

'Stipe football champion!' I said and his grin grew even wider. It was the best birthday he'd ever had. For he's a jolly good fellow.

And so
say all
of us.

A Swastika Pointing the Wrong Way Was Probably Drawn by a Fascist

Maqsood has got it, eureka. After studying his file and combing through half the laws of Belgium, he has come to the conclusion that becoming Belgian is unbelievably easy: you just have to marry a Belgianess.

A *Belgische*.

All he needs is a woman, preferably with the full quota of ears and limbs, and then he can get his papers in order. No more bothersome interrogations at the Aliens Department, where you queue up for three hours for an interview that lasts five minutes at the most, with an interpreter who mistranslates everything and an outcome that was decided before they asked the first question. Maqsood was so overwhelmed by the realization that it was possible for him to acquire legal status in bed that at dinner he couldn't eat a bite. I'm always glad to see Maqsood upset, it means I get enough to eat. The cook insisted that it was tuna with rice, both on my plate *and* in the bowl Maqsood gave me.

Until it starts growling again, I decide to concentrate on my stomach and enjoy. Afterwards I'll point out to Maqsood that his gut has been ripped open and his eyes are in such a state that it looks like someone's plonked two scoops of strawberry ice cream down in his sockets, and that men like that aren't exactly in demand. For the time being though, the poor sod is living in the delusion that he will soon be marrying a Flemish wench who will fry herring for him on Fridays and cut up six or seven potatoes to make home-made chips every Sunday. He's already asked me to be his witness at the town hall. Gladly.

Western women are still won in discotheques. At least, according to Maqsood, the playboy of Kashmir, and the usual procedure is apparently to select a girl, march straight up with an expression of complete confidence on your face, ask her for a light or the time, and then buy her a drink. The most expensive one on the menu, sweet and bubbly, with a slice of lime and a straw. And alcoholic. Until they're boozed up, Western women tend to act like Western men. You wait patiently for a slow number – those in a hurry can request one of those cloying songs in the meantime, after all, a dj's only purpose in life is to bring people together – and then, while shuffling over the dance floor with your hips swaying, one hand on her shoulder and the hand of God in her trousers (not too deep, just a couple of millimetres under the elastic), you politely ask her to marry you. The most important thing with a Western woman is to convince her from the word go that she won't have to wear a burqa, you won't hit her, you won't insist on her having more than five children and you'll help with the washing-up. Her answer will be a firm no, but you should never forget that, when they say no, Western women almost always mean yes. And once you've crossed that threshold, you can set a date and get measured up for your wedding suit.

Thanks to this solid theoretical basis, Maqsood succeeded in getting beaten up on his first campaign of conquest. Still, it can't be proven in black and white that his broken wrist was a direct consequence of his strategy, he simply failed to ascertain that his target was already in possession of another – unfortunately more muscular – man, the kind of guy who builds up his circle of friends at the gym. You always have teething problems.

Nowadays Maqsood breaks the ice by asking women to sign his plaster cast. And he's come to value my company during his hunting expeditions. After all, we only get one evening off a month, one lousy chance to flout the curfew and venture out into the testosterone-drenched Flemish night – after handing in a signed promise that we won't come back drunk. *Vamos!*

Picking up a woman in a disco is not the biggest problem. The biggest problem is getting into a disco in the first place. Invariably there's a brick shithouse on the door – ten to one in sunglasses, even if it's three in the morning, even if it's fifteen years since the sun last shone on the bruiser's head – and he stands there glibly insisting that it's a private club or full up, or you're wearing the wrong shoes, or you need a moustache to go inside, or it's a theme night and everyone has to be dressed up as a giraffe, or that admission costs 800 Belgian francs (being 20 future euros) and 1,200 francs for non-members (being 104 Lithuanian litai, being 108,250 Rumanian lei). And meanwhile he's waving in gorgeous potential fiancées who don't hand over a penny and, on closer investigation, aren't even disguised as giraffes. Without a moustache between them. The only place in the whole neighbourhood where we can get in past the obligatory brick shithouse is the one club Maqsood no longer dares to enter. He's scared of getting his other wrist broken as well.

Thanks to his stubborn refusal to lose faith in humanity, Maqsood has spent his entire life being fucked up the arse by the entire human race. He's a total innocent – and therefore perfect husband material – but the road to a wife is paved with dangers he is always completely oblivious to. If we pass a pub in which, theoretically, his future flame could be sitting bored at the bar puffing away at a cigarette, constantly racing off to the ladies' to touch up her lips, grinning sweetly at the barman, who is too busy pouring beers fast enough to make sure his customers keep grinning...then Maqsood is convinced that all the people in the pub have been awaiting his arrival for years. 'Look, there, friendly people!'

That's not something you see every day, so I ask where.

'There, at the door of that pub, they're waving to us.'

'Keep walking, Maqsood, that's the Hitler salute.'

And since there are thousands of different salutes, and people in the asocial Western world usually just ignore each other, Maqsood returns their attentions with a friendly Hitler salute of his own. And a smile. I also Hitler salute your mother and all your sisters. And then we get to test our aerobic fitness, pursued by fourteen single-minded skinheads. The pub in question was called the *Welkom*.

But a man who's set his sights on a wife-cum-passport is not easily deterred and Maqsood had vowed to get himself a woman before returning to the asylum centre. In the end we found an establishment without any sunglasses on guard duty. A poster on the door said, 'New Wave Party'.

New Wave, unless I'm very much mistaken, is the exact English translation of Bossa Nova, being sultry Brazilian dance music that sounds as if for centuries there's been a universally affordable cure for cancer, the kind of music that makes you want to swing your hips. You keep an invisible Hula-Hoop in motion while giving testosterone-drenched looks to a Hula-Hooper of the opposite sex. There's nothing else to it, and you walk out of the party tent and straight down the aisle. We opened the door. An ashen-faced kid at a kitchen table asked us for eighty francs admission, four Bulgarian levas. The proceeds of the show, he assured us, were going towards new corrugated iron for the roof of the scout hall. Congratulations. The dance floor was completely deserted, unless we were willing to take into account three almost stationary, witch-like apparitions in black rags. Maqsood was wearing a tie with embroidered cartoon characters and I had fished my whitest tennis socks out of the washing machine for the occasion, but still we didn't feel at home.

'Did someone die here?' But the barman had either gone deaf from years of working in this loud gloomy music or couldn't be bothered answering. And the disc jockey had apparently just heard from a reliable source that God didn't exist, because when we requested a solid swingalong number like Michael Jackson's *Billy Jean*, all the world's misery suddenly convened in the middle of his face. Things picked up for a moment when the godless killjoy pulled something out of his record box that actually got twenty people out under the mirror ball. The German singer kept repeating that he wanted to be a polar bear – I'd like to be a polar bear, I'd like to be a polar bear, at the cold Pole, I'd like to be a polar bear – and that all the way through the refrain. Besides arms, we now saw the odd foot moving in a suggestion of a dance step and with every passing moment, I felt sadder about them not letting us in to the giraffe party.

'I don't understand,' I told Maqsood. 'Would you like to be a polar bear?'

Maqsood didn't understand anything anymore, least of all the fact that you had to pay here to take a leak. 77 Slovenian tolars per piddle. 'Why do they want to make money off that? It's my piss!'

Anyway, we went home, to Block 4, in the cold – it's still much too cold to sneak into a container

– and decided to postpone the wedding ceremony a little longer. Better luck next month. If we're still walking around here. If we're still walking around.

Sheltering in Eddy Merckx Country

Arsehole of the day is Ifeanyi Akwuegbu who can't ride a bike properly.

The election of Ifeanyi to arsehole of the day is the first notable fact on a Tuesday that is so unnoteworthy that it might just as well have been a Wednesday or a Friday. The second prominent feature in the landscape of our boredom is that General Tomatski received a deportation order but decided to jump before he was pushed. He disappeared last night. We all know that Tomatski paid the mafia a substantial sum for seven attempts to smuggle him to England. He still had three attempts left to go. In the confusion of his flight he left a bottle of whisky in his room, and in the corridor an intense debate is now raging about who has the most right to claim it. The debate is whispered, a wall of quiet mumbling, because when it comes to alcohol the house rules are implacable: anyone found in a state of drunkenness will be ejected from the centre immediately and without exception. The incident also goes on your file, thus ruining your chances with the Aliens Department. Inasmuch as you had any chances in the first place.

For now, we don't get any further than agreeing to decide possession of the bottle over a game of chess. We could also put it to a democratic vote, at least, if anyone on our corridor understood what those things mean: 'democratic', 'vote'.

Sad lives too are subject to change, Ifeanyi has provided ample proof of that, and what changes constantly is the life, not the sadness. Until yesterday we were able to go to reception to borrow a bicycle, or at least, something with pedals, a seat and handlebars. We were able to get our minds off things now and then by riding into the village. Window-shopping was enough, it doesn't take much to fuel a dream. Most people use the bikes to go to Mass on Sundays. And since nothing much goes on around here except the occasional fight between a Chechen and a black, with a lot of cigarettes being bet on the Chechen, it can only make you more Catholic. Some guys I know make a habit of attending every available celebration of the Eucharist, from early Mass to midnight Mass, plus baptisms and funerals. But Ifeanyi has put an end to all that. Now there's a chance that we'll have to cover the whole distance to the village by foot, which can only lead to a drastic reduction in the number of the faithful.

It's like this: Ifeanyi comes from one of those African holes that can safely be considered the provincial capital because there's a well with filthy water. As long as you kick it hard enough, a donkey is the most efficient means of transport. The greatest dilemma in Ifeanyi's hometown concerns that same donkey, an animal created by African gods with a dual purpose in mind: trusty steed and roast dinner. If you eat the donkey, you have to do without your racing machine. If you ride it, you go hungry. Before leaving his native soil, Ifeanyi had never seen a bicycle, let alone a bike path. No surprize considering that the apex of cycle racing in all of Black Africa is the Tour de Burkina Faso: just follow your nose, the start is the last straight line, a bit like life itself. Anyway, it's hard to find anyone there who can take a corner on a bike. All well and good, and after reaching Europe, Ifeanyi was introduced to the wondrous vehicle. In all honesty, I must admit that he was surprizingly quick to find his balance on the rusty thing. It would be easy enough to laugh at him for dismounting at every corner, but I know of very few people who have the courage to learn to ride a bicycle at forty-five. I wouldn't want them putting me on a camel at my age either. Hats off on that account! The unfortunate thing is that Ifeanyi thinks that the middle of the road is by far the easiest place to ride. The car drivers annoy themselves a triple ulcer and beep furiously, convincing Ifeanyi that the Belgians are altogether the nicest people in the whole world so that he answers their beeping with two rows of shining white teeth. He would have rather waved, but he really was wiser to keep both hands on the handlebars.

Asylum seekers are not insured, not for

anything, for bugger-all. If a deranged fool takes it into his head to run us down, it's up to us to glue our body parts back together again. And we can pay for the super-glue while we're at it.

And so the management has decided that from now on we have to take a bicycle test, theoretical and practical, all equal before the law. So that everyone knows that a traffic light is not a Christmas decoration. They need to be sure of our bicycle skills. It's ridiculous. Are we supposed to slalom around traffic cones, corner, brake, ride uphill, ride downhill, with light, without light, ring the broken bell, pump up the tyre and put the chain back on under the watchful eye of the centre's managers, who meanwhile assess our navigational skills? Anyone who fails to graduate with honours will be excluded from borrowing a bike. Childhood is pleasant because it's over, no one is grateful to Ifeanyi for making us all feel like we're suddenly seven years old again.

Ifeanyi may not understand traffic signs, and he might have been chosen arsehole of the day by unanimous decision, but he can still cut the knot when it comes to allocating a bottle of whisky. It's because he thinks in terms of distribution rather than allocation. His suggestion is to play chess for shots. The winner of the game throws back a glass of whisky and gets to take on the next candidate. Anna, the whore, is absolutely delighted by this luminous idea and, after a little scheming amongst ourselves, we all agree that Anna will play Ifeanyi in the first game and I will act as judge for the duration of the tournament.

Anna has well-known skills that are highly valued and rewarded with cigarettes, but she is not a good chess player. She loses with white in next to no time and Ifeanyi triumphantly torments his body with a stiff drink, thrown back in one gulp. I can't help but wonder if he actually likes the stuff.

Ifeanyi just keeps winning, defeating an Albanian, the Algerian lawyer (although very narrowly), a Kosovar, a Chechen, a Serb, a Croat, a Gypsy without papers and another Albanian... in that order. He could have taken on a Korean as well, but the bottle is empty and his liver is working overtime.

The smirking losers congratulate Ifeanyi on his masterful moves, but the biggest prize is yet to come, seeing as Anna is already on her way to the office to inform the management that Mr. Ifeanyi Akwuegbu is shit-faced drunk in Block 4.

The Transmission of the Sigh

Lidia doesn't need to shout, she can talk calmly, almost as quietly as when she talks to me at night and thousands of miles away her voice can still be heard. She's sitting here in my room – Room 26, Block 4 – but at the same time she's also in the middle of a conversation in a mountain village on the Illyrian-Pelasgian border. Telecommunication is a marvellous thing, and the ability to be constantly amazed by it is a habit we should cherish.

Look at her sitting here on the edge of my bed wearing little more than knickers and a pink T-shirt while her voice effortlessly travels the enormous distance to the village of her birth. She doesn't even need to squeeze into a container to get there. If I didn't know better, I would hold my nose to the receiver to smell the wheat on the other end of the line, the dust, the brown coal, the sulphur, the lanes with all their scrawny cats...her roots.

For the first time since arriving here, Lidia has phoned home to talk to her mother. Or rather, since her mother's house does not contain any marvellous devices, she's phoned the village post office to ask them to call her mother to the phone.

'Who did you say you are?... Yes... And who would you like to speak to?... Yes... No idea, madam, there was shooting again last night and a few houses burnt down, I'll go see if we can find her. Can you hold the line?'

Far away in this same instant someone leaves a post office. Far away in this instant someone walks past the rubble and asks a passer-by if he knows where Lidia's mother is – alive, if possible – because she's wanted on the phone. Lidia sighs. Somewhere faraway from here, and in this same instant, a receiver is lying on a table in a post office. And from that receiver this sigh emerges. Does anyone hear it? Someone in the queue for stamps maybe? And do they sigh as well, considering the contagious nature of sighs?

There are two possibilities. Either someone now drops a knife, immediately stopping her potato peeling and chicken plucking to race to the post office in record speed. Or else the chicken is still alive and there's no one left to race to the post office.

A squeaking door. Footsteps. Banging. Crackling.

'Lidia, is that you?'

'Mama, is that you?'

Two voices embrace. They do that somewhere in the cosmos, where satellites distribute telephone conversations around the world. A moving thought. But too bad for the chicken.

'Where are you now, girl? Did the trip go well?'

Mother doesn't need to worry, the trip couldn't have been better. The smugglers had organized everything perfectly, the forged documents were very professional, the borders a mere formality. Once they'd got past the first danger zone, they were able to swap the trucks for an air-conditioned coach that had been placed at their disposal. They stopped regularly, more or less every three hours, at service areas where they were able to drink coffee and stretch their legs. And at night they were put to bed in hotels ranging in quality from three to five stars. There were bars, swimming pools, saunas, and breakfast with croissants and freshly squeezed orange juice. After five days, they reached the coast, where the ferry brought them to the promised land in just a couple of hours. She felt a little bit seasick, but other than that there weren't any discomforts worth mentioning on the whole trip.

'Your cousin will be glad to hear that. Ruslan. They're looking for him. They think he killed a Muslim and he wants to get away before they get their hands on him. I'll tell him you had a good trip, he'll be glad to hear it. And where are you calling from now, girl?'

She's standing in a telephone box in the middle of London. The Thames is flowing by on her left, and she can see Big Ben and the Houses of Parliament. It's a beautiful city, London. The people are all friendly, and fortunately most of them speak English. She's got a bar job. ('No,

Mother, it's not what you think, it's a respectable bar with respectable customers who talk about Shakespeare and the stock exchange.') She's making good money and can afford to eat a hamburger at McDonald's every day. The Marlboros here taste better than at home. She's living in a flat, she's got a cleaning lady who doesn't nose through her cupboards, and she's already enrolled at a school to complete her studies.

'Ruslan will be glad to hear it. Ruslan, your cousin, they're looking for him. They think he murdered a Muslim, but I know he didn't do it. Ruslan doesn't do things like that, but what difference does that make? Those Muslims will never believe it anyway, they just want to take revenge on the first innocent sheep to come their way, that's what they're like. But I'll tell him, that you're in London, that everything's fine there, that you got there without any trouble and that he should look you up. Have you got an address?'

Number 10 Downing Street, can she write that down?

Mother can't write English, but thinks she'll be able to remember it.

'Ruslan will be glad to hear it. He'll be leaving soon to get away from the Muslims who unjustly accuse him of murdering their brothers. I'll tell him you're living in London, Number 10 Towny Street, and that he can stay with you until he's got a job and a flat of his own. Ruslan is good with wood, maybe he can find a job there in a furniture factory. Can I tell him that, girl, that he can stay with you?'

Sure.

'Can you sleep at night, now there's no bombs falling next to your bed?'

'Is everything all right with you, Mother?'

'Your father and I used to live next to a busy railway. People used to wonder how we could sleep through all that rattling and clanging. But when we finally moved to the cottage you were born in, we lay awake night after night. We missed the noise of the trains, we'd lost something familiar... Is everything going well?'

Sure. Very well. Things could be better, of course. But sayings like that seem to be reserved for people who couldn't be worse off.

'And the weather? What's the weather like in London? What clothes should Ruslan bring with him? He wants to flee. The Muslims have already beaten the stuffing out of him and they told him it's not going to stop there. They've shown him the knife they're going to cut his throat with. Gangsters, that's what they are.'

Shut up, you senile old bag.

'Mother, listen, I'm standing here in a telephone box, there's people waiting and I just ordered a taxi to take me to work. It could arrive any minute now, I've got to hang up...'

'...Ah, girl, if only you knew how often and how hard I've prayed for this, that you'd land on your feet and have a good life. You still pray, don't you? You remember to thank God every day? You haven't forgotten that you should use prayer like antibiotics, before and after dinner? I'm so happy to hear your voice again. If they start shooting again tonight, at least I'll know they can't get you anymore, that you're safe and sound.'

Lidia hangs up. In the cosmos two voices withdraw from their embrace.

'That woman has never seen a taxi close-up in her life. She probably thinks the driver will wait for me for hours,' she tells me. 'At least Mother will sleep well tonight.'

If we didn't have mothers, we wouldn't need to tell lies.

In this instant, somewhere, her mother is singing while plucking a chicken.

In this instant, here, Lidia and I sit on the edge of my bed waiting for the postman to bring news from the other side of the barbed wire. We count the minutes until it's time for dinner to take our minds off things, and Lidia hopes that it will be chicken, or something that tastes like it.

Not Much Beats an Unhappy Marriage

Maqsood has got it, eureka. It must have temporarily slipped his mind that he is now in capitalist hemispheres, that this is Europe, where you can buy anything, whether it's cars or wives. The newspapers are full of women who put themselves on offer, little birds begging to be ringed, and whereas he started off not knowing how to strike up a conversation with one woman, now he can't choose between hundreds and hundreds of languishing 'personals'. It's a harem, and it takes Maqsood a whole week to pick out the ones with the most charms. Here: a hairdresser, 48, divorced, very young and open character, pleasant company, super-cute, she hopes you have charisma and can enjoy life. There: a manager, 33, divorcee, beautiful, of course, she expects the love of her life to be dynamic and unprejudiced. And this one: Raquel is her name, 45, she is looking for a very sweet boyfriend around the same age – 'I am five foot nine, slim, blond and like having fun'. Ever met anyone who dislikes having fun? Cross the bimbo off! Or Tanya, 32, from Ghent, five foot seven, short blond hair and green eyes and, uh-oh, an eleven year old son. Dump the mummy. And what to make of the twenty-seven year old teacher from Brussels: single, very beautiful young lady, brunette, beautiful smile, extremely charming; she will seduce you. 'Blonde Ms. seeks SWM to 40 w/w.o. kid. NS/ND. Dendermonde area. Likes film, mus, cuis, trav...' Difficult, cryptograms like that.

Capitalism is a wonderful invention and the only disadvantage is that you need money to participate in it. They call it investment. Cash flow. Bingo. Jackpot. *Nasdaq*. Those are glorious words, expletives that can, in this land of milk and mayonnaise, even be applied to acquiring a wife. And not forgetting the passport that comes with her – *abracadabra*.

Maqsood lays down three thousand in coins to join a dating service: 47 Latvian lats, 102,583 Korean wons, 123 Singapore dollars. And in return he receives a magazine full of enticing girls' names and gets to spend two Sunday afternoons at Dancehall Cassanova dancing with a long line of singles. One drink is included in the price, the dress code is stylish and tidy.

The passport justifies the courting, Maqsood invests his last three thousand and circles the ads where he thinks the word should finally become flesh.

We see a destitute Maqsood return from Dancehall Cassanova. Not one fish took the bait, but he now knows the jargon of the go-between.

Not unattractive: stands for enormously ugly.

Voluptuous: stands for fleshy, jellyfish-like, thousand-lobed and hundred-lipped, a woman with a pouch under her chin, four spare tyres, varicose veins on her legs, sebaceous cysts on her neck, as wide as the Bering Strait.

Sporty: a bint who gets exhausted when she leaves the car in the garage for once and rides her bike to work, but spends three minutes a day pedalling her home trainer; or a half hour a week doing yoga with an equally pathetic girlfriend while spiritually concentrating on the kilos in the hope they'll disappear.

Divorced: really does stand for divorced, but also indicates that it makes complete sense for a man to have left a woman like this, not even a dog could stick it out with her for long.

If the advertizement does not mention an age, the single woman is a pensioner.

If the advertizement does not mention a profession, she is unemployed.

If the advertizer does not care whether or not you have children, she is such a social defect that she couldn't even chat to the neighbours about the weather, not even if it's been raining non-stop for seven weeks, not even if it's liquid manure falling out of the sky, two inches a day, and although she may want company down the rest of life's pathway – because that's what they call it – she doesn't care who it is, he can have sixty kids if necessary, half of them hyperactive, or retarded, as long as she gets to avoid dying alone, as long as she has a hand to hold when the nurse comes to tell her that the great journey is about to begin because it's time for them to switch off the machine. Not that there's anything wrong with that, but Maqsood is looking for another type. Sorry.

If a sweet-tempered lady is looking for a gentleman who has had the benefit of a university education, then it's very tempting to think that she wants to spend her days with an intellectual equal, but the depressing reality – after all, that's why it *is* the reality – is that the cow is too lazy to lift a finger and is looking for somebody loaded. So that she can live it up for once, go to a beauty salon at last, get mud smeared all over her mug, and cucumber on her eyes, and clay on her blubbery belly, and putty in her pores, or fibreglass in her boobs. So she can go on holiday somewhere where they put the right paper umbrellas in the right cocktails. And so she can afford a cleaning lady to do the house, what are we saying, so she can afford to give a cleaning lady a kick up the bum when she's forgotten to sweep the fluff out from under the wardrobe, so that she can recruit a new cleaning lady to kick.

Sensitive: stands for hysterical. And ten to one, slim means anorexic.

Foodie: stands for someone who sees the wok as the pinnacle of the culinary arts. And thinks that cheese smells good, but men's feet stink.

Sense of humour: a woman who does laugh a lot, but unfortunately never knows why.

Maqsood is disillusioned and considers seeking asylum in a communist country if they deport him. His last, faint hope of finding a woman and a passport rests in the ad he himself gets to place in the dating service magazine for his squandered 100,000 wons.

MAQSOOD exot. boy, 32, urgently seeks unsporty, insensitive, humourless YL for new start in life. S/D, no kids. Dislikes film, good food, trav. No foreigners!

'Sailing Is Necessary, Living Is Not.' (Plutarch)

The little man standing in front of the map of Europe looked funny to me. A goody-goody scientist who had somehow had the luck, or maybe the misfortune, to stumble into a job as a weatherman. He had a moustache that didn't look good on him at all and which he undoubtedly grew after standing in front of the mirror one day and ascertaining that he didn't look good without a moustache. He wore his suit the way children wear a Communion suit: uncomfortable but proud.

While he explained the free movement of the winds with angular gestures, his sleeves slid up – bought too short. A slight stir passed through our television room when, with a measured smile, he predicted that the temperatures would finally creep up above zero. Instead of drifting down, so-and-so-many millimetres of precipitation would come pissing and dripping out of the sky. But what mattered was that the cold snap was over. No warnings for roads or bridges.

For plenty of people here, this weather report is a wake-up call. All plans for England had frozen with the puddles, but that's coming to an end. Lidia asks me whether I'm willing to stowaway with her in a ship's belly. Her dreams are thawing and that's dangerous. She's a minor, no one can touch her. She can stay here for at least two more years, she doesn't even need to stand on a landmine on her way to the shop to get some bread, why should she risk her life for an existence that starts every day in front of the telly with a bowl of cornflakes and ends in a bed in a house that is quaint in its way but too small for a bloke who's just knocked back pint after pint of Newcastle Brown at the pool table because his football team neglected to score? The English are stark staring mad, doesn't she know that? They drive on the wrong side of the road and they think golf and cricket are exciting. Lady Di was the most beautiful woman they had ever seen, gossip is a national pastime, killing foxes is a sign of wealth, and they take their minds off unemployment by showing films about unemployment in their cinemas. Is that where her happiness lies?

First, she has no desire to twiddle her thumbs until her eighteenth birthday. And second, she has even less desire to return to Go without collecting four thousand Belgian francs. I understand. I can get numbers one and two into my head, but the third – that she's thinking of me instead of a boozed-up Anglo-Saxon – that's a different story. I'd like to swallow but I can't find any spit.

As bitter as it may sound, nowhere am I easier

to love than in an asylum centre. When I was a press photographer, women found me too cynical.

For now. She loves me for now. Because I don't need to come back exhausted from my job, because I've still got a reason to be sad. How she'll react to my persistent melancholic moods when everything is going well, I have no idea, and neither does she. Sometimes I'm too lazy to replace an empty toilet roll. Will she be able to put up with that? Can she put up with me gnashing my teeth when I'm asleep? She can now, but will she be able to keep it up? My farts stink, I peel off my toenails. I never get to bed on time, I never get up on time, and I have a horror of concerts and theatre performances. Because thunderous applause sounds like a horde of AK-47's. Because my sister died before my eyes during thunderous applause. I stuff crisps into my mouth and spill half of them in the process, I've never correctly estimated how much spaghetti to cook for two people, and I can be very rude when someone tries to explain my character traits to me.

I see prayers rolling by in Lidia's eyes, supplications.

I close my eyes and see her as she just was, in her knickers. There are stars and comets on those knickers. It's not the kind of underwear I would buy for myself, but she looks wonderful in it. Three days ago a comet hit the earth – next to my bed, the third tile counting back from the end, to be precise – and, instead of ending, the world became more beautiful.

'I asked the director of the centre for

contraceptives,' she says, she who hurls the stars. 'Tomorrow I can see the doctor for an injection.'

Apparently we're a couple and the management knew before I did...

England. It's true that I've learnt over the last few weeks to stop thinking about my future, I've postponed all thought of it. One day I left my village, knowing exactly where I was going: Vita Nova. I knew what I was after and when I crossed the border at Bobrowniki, I realized that happiness was coming ever closer. But since then I've fallen into a coma and the longer I wait for permission to remain in this country, the more I forget. I was in the perfect present – without past or future – until Lidia dragged me back to consciousness, and I can't say she's wrong. You'd have to be mad to wait for a decision that besides being two years too late could also be to your disadvantage. If it's happiness you were pursuing, why hang around for months on end grumbling in an asylum centre? England. The word alone rips my stomach open, but if all the other countries keep refusing us, what choice do we have?

'Christmas!' and out of her mouth it's more divine than ever, 'Christmas! If you ask me, that's the best time to risk it. The whole country's running at half steam. The harbour police would rather be inside with a cup of tea and a piece of cake than outside doing inspections. The customs officers don't have their heart in it. They'd rather be home stuffing themselves with turkey.'

She'd do well in sales, she doesn't mention the

minuses. The days that you could find a ship owner who was willing to smuggle you over are long gone, or as good as. If customs finds stowaways on his ship, they'll suspect him of people smuggling. He'll have to pay horrific fines and his crew will waste precious time in front of a noisy police typewriter trying to prove the company's innocence. Rest assured: if the ship's cook finds you crouching behind the hamburger meat, they'll chuck you overboard. That will save the crew a lot of bother. No one will ever know, it's not as if anyone's going to miss you. Maybe a fishing boat will trawl up one of your feet in a net, somewhere between a rusty bicycle and school of gasping tuna, but that really is all they'll find.

Has she ever actually seen a cargo hold close-up? It's not the kind of place you jump into, not unless you want to end up spread over the floor. In some of those rusty old tubs they pile up seven or more containers on top of each other, that's how deep they are. And there you wait, if you're lucky, with just enough room to scratch your nose. You wait for them to cast off, the engines start to pound, so loud that hairline cracks start spreading over your skull. You've left, the journey to freedom has begun... And then? How can you say with any certainty that the ship is going the right way? Okay, you stood on the quay, you read the name of an English city or company on the bow and slipped into the hold unnoticed. You think, bingo, you've made it, but the company has to make the ship pay, so they send it to Rotterdam first to pick up some Gouda, and after that it's got seven containers of cheddar to drop off in a port in Norway. The ship stops there for a while for minor repairs, a slight delay, the sailors go on shore to forget the emptiness of the seas for a while in the arms of a siren. How long have you been standing there, crammed in between those containers? Did you bring enough food with you, enough to drink? Haven't you frozen yet? Haven't you dehydrated yet from the heat of the engines? The sea rocks the boat, you puke. Because it's the umpteenth day in a row that you've been going up and down, up and down, up and down – sometimes a bit less, other times much more. That's more than a land-lover like you can stand, you can't stop spewing. You're going to die and screaming won't help. There's no one to hear.

'You don't want to come with me.'

'That's not what I said. I want to make you aware of the risks, a ship is not a truck.'

'That's what I said, you don't want to come with me.'

'I have to think about it seriously, Lidia. Christmas is too much of a rush, that's five days away, damn it.'

There is a silence that reminds me of earlier silences, after which I saw a woman's heels in the doorway. Her name was Bethina, and she set the stakes as high as Lidia now. Sometimes I think I left *her*, not my country.

'There's also such a thing as a tunnel to England. Sounds safer. I know some who made it.' I'm actually trying to talk myself out of my memories, but it's already too late.

'How good are you at saying goodbye?'

I look at the universe, the stars, the comets. The Little Bear. Three days ago I kissed it. How good am I at saying goodbye? I'm a past master. And worse every time.

She pulls up her jeans. A cloud slides across the sun.

Posthumorous Work

Opinions differ as to the quality of the razor blades they supply us with here and that's a good thing, because imagine if we all had similar ideas about razor blades, then we would rarely, if ever, talk about razor blades. And it's a relief to talk about razor blades, in my opinion, because then you're not all standing around crapping on about home. Unless you're stupid enough to keep talking to the same people for too long, because eventually someone is bound to say that the razor blades were better at home. It's important to keep your brains supple, to force yourself to think about things and discuss them with others. Disagreeing about the quality of razor blades is a question of survival – it sustains the will to survive. Someone who stops considering a razor blade a worthy subject of conversation is already losing their grip on existence. In this sense no one is amused to hear that Sedi has delivered the definitive proof of the merit of our razor blades by using one to slice open an artery. He was still breathing when we found him – more out than in, but hell, he was breathing – and Shaukat, who sees entrepreneurial potential in everything, immediately bet a full pack of cigarettes that Sedi would survive *this* suicide attempt as well.

Now Shaukat's being a pain in the neck because he doesn't have any cigarettes left and hardly got a look in when Sedi's things were being shared out more or less honestly. Prosinecki actually got the best deal of all by claiming Sedi's Hawaiian shirts, now at least he's got something *really* ugly to put on when he has to go to Brussels to defend his asylum application. Because besides the quality of our razor blades, consensus was also reached recently on the fact that that you're better off not looking too stylish at the Aliens Department. They could decide that you have it way too good here on earth and that, as a result, there can't possibly be any reason to allow your application. Just look at that Kosovar who went there for an interview recently in a tie and a leather jacket, a complete pot of shell-pink gel in his coiffure and his nails trimmed, not chewed. A week later they put him on the plane in his tie and leather jacket and he got to chew his nails while looking out over the natural beauties of the Ardennes. But there are tricks for that too, Maqsood claims. 'The Belgian government doesn't have the pesos to fly all those rejected asylum seekers back by Lear jet, so they put all their reject refugees on an ordinary scheduled flight with a bunch of holiday-makers. You just need to start ranting and raving and screaming blue murder and crying and screeching and yelling and shrieking and shitting. You'll give headaches to both the pilots and the passengers – who, after all, have paid through the nose for their smoke-free flight to the balmy Yugoslav coast – they won't be able to concentrate on the safety instructions or watch the videos, and the cabin crew will kick you straight off the plane. On a subsequent attempt to repatriate you, you repeat your theatrical tour de force, in the end it will cost the airline so many customers that they'll get sick of your crap and finally give you a boot up the arse and tell you to find your own way back. Something you, of course, promise to do.'

Not the most nutritious perhaps, but definitely the tastiest crust to be earned from Sedi's death is the one that fell into Pius's hands. As he shared a room with the unfortunate, he now sleeps alone. That won't last long, but while it does, he can enjoy.

Pius is an inconspicuous guy who rarely gets mixed up in discussions and never complains. The only thing Pius hates is Pius himself, which could indicate that he's not the most stupid person around. Insofar as his story can be considered watertight, he's got an enormous price on his head in his motherland for being an overly critical editor of the university magazine. The crossword puzzles he designed were apparently stuffed with secret messages to overthrow the government, and apparently that kind of thing is not allowed there. They're after his scalp, all the more since he's demonstrated that the government has nothing better to do than solve crossword puzzles.

Pius's story has the Aliens Department baffled. All the idiotic pieces fit together so nicely that they can't deport him on grounds of inconsistency. After gruelling deliberations, a narrow majority seems to have settled for indecision (the rest abstained), and Pius is now going into his fourteenth month as an asylum seeker. But from all outward appearances that doesn't seem to make him any crazier. The reason he hasn't flung himself off the frayed edge of the world after fourteen months' residence in No-Man's Land is a mystery whose solution is disappointingly simple: he acts like he's on holiday. And he does that with a fair degree of thoroughness, like a researcher, an explorer, as dedicated as if it's fallen to him to colour in the last blank patches on the map. He spends hours a day bent over graph paper scribbling it full of information about this virgin territory. *The Lovely Planet Guide: Problemski Hotel* is the title and it must qualify as the ultimate travel guide.

The Lovely Planet Guide: Problemski Hotel – the ultimate asylum centre guide in a paperback edition featuring...

Vivid descriptions of all the attractions, from the renowned showers to the bunk beds.

Reliable discussions of the best blocks to spend the night in, the television room, reception, the homework classes for the children – and much more.

Excursions to the toilets, the Aliens Department, container terminals and other destinations that are definitely worth a visit.

Colour maps showing places of interest and all recommended destinations (rated on a scale of one to five stars).

Background information and useful tips for the illegal residents of the future, including phone numbers to get in touch with slumlords and mafia bosses.

It doesn't include any crosswords. The shining example was Xavier de Maistre, an author who was subjected to forty-two days of house arrest after winning a sword duel and reported on a journey through his room (a smart fucker, Pius). Sometimes travel is a question of language: a day can look completely different when you replace the word refectory with the word restaurant. Considered superficially, you could take Pius's travel guide for a sarcastic intermezzo, but it does seem as though the author in question really means it. Relaxed, he shuffles to the showers in plastic flip-flops, the fluorescent yellow ones, usually worn by women whose shape makes it advantageous for them to wear conspicuous footwear that draws attention to their feet. He stands in the shower singing the way only holidaymakers at campsites can sing. I once prided myself on not knowing anyone who feels an urge to demonstrate their knowledge of operetta while rubbing suds into their hair, but Pius has changed all that. If the sun shines in the summer, he spreads his towel out on the hard cement of the inner courtyard and starts baking. It makes his days easier. Accordingly, his travel guide includes a chapter on which corners of the asylum centre get the most hours of sun annually, just for sun worshippers. People who like peace and quiet can find a brief summary of the ideal spots on page 40, and sex tourists are given directions on how to find Anna.

His masterpiece has progressed through three improved editions, printed in the computer class, but he can't find any takers. I think I'm the only one who was foolish enough to read the thing and even pay him a packet of cigarettes for it. I actually had no choice but to read his monstrosity – for some incomprehensible reason he had dedicated it to me, which is why I was kind of shocked when he refused to budge on his price of one packet of cigarettes. At the moment he's considering a new enterprize: the idea that postcards of the asylum centre would do well has taken root in his head. Everyone could write to the family they left behind without tying themselves in knots to explain what the centre actually looks like. The problem is a camera – Pius just can't pick one up cheap enough. I know the feeling.

Of course, Pius's eccentric behaviour is noticed. By Albanians who consider Pius so daft that he's not even worth bashing. And by Annick, whose psychological support is available every Thursday between three and four pm. She has a room here in restful colours that give me a headache, a chair that's bad for the back but good for the psyche, music that's too beautiful to make you forget your troubles, and magnificent eyes that are set perfectly behind her prescription lenses – artworks in a glass case. No one is obliged to visit her, and given that psychologists have a natural tendency to confront people with themselves, you really would have to to be pretty crazy to want to visit her in the first place. The problem is that there is so little going on here that Annick becomes a pleasant diversion. If I believe my own lies, if I forget that it's her job to chat pleasantly with other people, then I succeed in finding it pleasant to chat with Annick. Muslims or adherents of some other doctrine that claims that you shouldn't listen too much to women can have their peace of mind massaged on Tuesdays by André, also from three to five. Like Annick, André has a glass case on the bridge of his nose, the difference is that there's not much going on behind his lenses, which is why I prefer to see her. The first time was out of boredom. The second time was lust. Now I visit her weekly from misery. She says she can't help me. Making my misery grow, so that I need her even more in the week that follows. After some seven sessions in which I kept on telling her about my future, which is unrelentingly, classically gloomy, in which I wryly informed her that my thoughts are dominated by the unpleasant fact that I will very likely be murdered when they send me back to my country, she told me that there's not much I can do except prepare for my death. Every Thursday, from three to five, Annick helps me to prepare for my death. According to her, that clears the air. According to me, it gives me a hard-on.

Come five o'clock, it's dinnertime. Thursdays, immediately after my session with Annick, we get noodles. Being prepared for death does make it easier to shovel the muck in.

Whereas I was first seen as a wimp for lowering myself to a headshrinker's mumbo-jumbo, quite a few people have now followed my example. I even need to book in time to assure myself of my hour's psychologizing. It's because Annick officially banished all doubts about Pius by declaring him nutso. She put it down in black and white, admittedly in masked terms, to impress the stamp wielders of the Aliens Department. Madmen are sick. And somewhere, in some legislation, an eightieth clause of a seventh section of a footnote to a footnote of a postscript forbids the deportation of seriously ill asylum seekers. In other words, Pius has got it made. He is facing a future full of charming nurses who loathe and detest their jobs and stuff him full of masses of pills at breakfast until he's too dopey to enjoy their charms. He'll spend his Sunday afternoons in pyjamas, strolling through a garden filled with white aprons, and he'll be able to earn his own cigarettes, at least if he has any talent for macramé. But that might still be better than having to go back to Mozambique, where, just by adding his fingerprint to a piece of paper without a spelling mistake, he'd make the development index shoot up.

For those who have nothing to lose and consider macramé a better option than martyrdom, following in Pius's footsteps is a logical choice. Shaukat, who honestly wouldn't look bad in a strait-jacket, seized the cow by the udders by immediately informing Annick, 'I am mad.'

That tactic didn't help.

Ifeanyi then tried it by declaring in mid-session that his main problem was that he was completely normal, but that too proved a little too transparent.

Tomorrow a bus is taking Pius to the home. We'll help him to pack his shirt and his two pairs of underpants. And at the barbed wire, we'll wave until he disappears out of sight. And Pius, Pius will smile, as ambiguously as lunatics always smile. And then we'll go and pull up a few more weeds, punch someone in the face out of boredom, get bored out of boredom.

Rocky III

Too much happiness is bad as well. Assisting at the birth of the baby a rapist had left in Martina's womb was less of a problem than I had expected. The problem was murdering the little tyke afterwards.

Martina was already about seven months gone – the being inside her was very much present and kicking for attention – before she figured out that she was absolutely sure she didn't want to keep it. After the tasteless conception and the missed period that followed, she immediately sank into a state of apathy, pure self-preservation, and acted as if everything was just fine. Then she was seized for a while by an atavistic remnant of maternal and other instincts that have left their mark on human chemistry and had her tidying her nest and scraping plaster off the walls to eat it up. This was followed by a recalcitrant period of fanatical self-mutilation. During her smuggling trip to Belgium she was too busy to think about an abortion and by the time she finally found her feet in the asylum centre and was sure she didn't want the baby, it was already too late to find a doctor willing to burn his fingers on a case like hers. There are plenty of women in the asylum centre who grew up in the bannat of sorcery and know how apply a comical feel for theatre to ward off head colds, tumours and pregnancy – tips and recipes for abortive syrups galore – but that devil's spawn wasn't budging and grew and grew, until Wednesday night, when it broke her waters with a single head butt.

Martina's plan wasn't the kind of thing you wanted to trumpet about, but a few people, including me, were in the know and had promised to help. It was important that none of the staff caught whiff of the delivery, that no one heard a cry from an early labour pain, because that would mean a trip to the hospital, where they'd use a toolbox and medical nuts and bolts and whatever other ice-cold gear it took to drag the kid out of her and keep it alive, because all unwanted life is holy. A few of us men took up positions in the corridor to distract the night watchman in case he showed any signs of wanting to inspect Block 4. Maqsood was a specialist at acting like his appendix had burst – groaning with pain, he was capable of demanding the attention of all of reception. I myself had once assisted at the birth of a calf, and in our corridor that was far and away the most relevant prior experience, so it was up to me to help with the birth. I didn't mention that I had also killed chickens – that was a task I preferred leaving to someone else. Lidia, who was born at the last birth she attended, trusted to her female intuition and promised to lend a hand. She didn't have much choice. Since she shared a room with Martina, she wouldn't be getting much sleep anyway. There were enough people around the place with experience in the field, but for various reasons they couldn't be trusted. The Somali woman in Block 6, for instance, had given birth so many times that it seemed as if she just squeezed the kids straight out of her tubes, but she would undoubtedly refuse to help this baby's fate along a little afterwards.

The weak link in our team, and we realized this all too well, was Dmitry. An Albanian. Since the child's father was an Albanian, Martina insisted that the baby should be killed by an Albanian as well. She thought that was correct, historically speaking. It was her idea of reparation. We had to promise him a lot of money (cigarettes weren't enough), but in the end Dmitry consented. He wouldn't see the cash until another month had gone by without it leaking out – you can never be too sure. And, as I said, on Wednesday night the moment had come.

Lidia woke me from a dream of snowy mountains, ten minutes later the whole team was in position. We were equipped with buckets and mops, which gave us a sense of being ready for anything.

I used to hear my aunts trying to outdo each other with outrageous stories about labour and birth, during which my uncles would leave the house so that they could maintain the delusion that men were tougher than women. Some of them had to push for days on end, litres of blood and fluid dripped out onto the floor before they so much as caught a glimpse of the baby. They didn't give up, not even when they tore open with a loud ripping sound. They would rather die then give up their baby. This was the moment in which I stopped understanding women and became an adult. My father's oldest sister always came out on top because she had given birth to my most obnoxious cousin during a flood, all alone, sitting on a bough of a tree. I too seem to have given my mother a hard time during my entry into the world, giving her the credentials to hold her head high when discussing female matters at tea parties. The morning after the family's expansion with yet another rumbling tummy, the mother would be back in the fields, because it wasn't just themselves, they wanted the earth to be productive as well. I had learnt a lot of things from those stories, but with Martina I didn't notice any of them. She didn't produce the sound of a piglet having its throat cut, she didn't even groan like a door. It didn't take hours and hours and hours before we solemnly snipped the umbilical cord with a pair of scissors. This was a woman who couldn't wait to get rid of her baby – that much was obvious. It took about ninety minutes and, suddenly, I was standing there with a kid in my arms. A boy, but I didn't think it necessary to inform Martina of the sex, it probably wouldn't have interested her too much. Thinking back on it now, I'm afraid I stood there too long with that little boy in my arms. But that baby was looking at me and I was looking at that baby. I was the first person he got to see, which must have come as a shock, and Dmitry would be the last one he'd get to study in this vale of tears. Dmitry was standing in the corner of the room and to me he seemed to be looking kind of pale, there wasn't a tint of pink left in his face. I handed him the child, now it was up to him.

You could have at least expected him to have thought about how to do the job, we were paying him well enough for it, but the jerk just asked what he was supposed to do. What was he supposed to do? Twist its bloody neck. Or smother it under a pillow. Or choke it. What was he asking *me* for? I said, 'What are you waiting for, man? Are you going to help it to the other world or aren't you?' But no, the macho started to sob, so that in the end you started feeling sorrier for him than you did for the mother. We had a problemski: he couldn't bring himself to do it, it reminded him of his own flesh and blood, the baby he had been forced to leave behind when he fled, he dished up the whole story, including all the details, and Dmitry was a complete write-off. Before it had time to sink in properly, I was standing there again with the little fellow in my hands, not knowing what to do with him.

Kootchy, kootchy, koo.

'You don't think *I'm* going to do it? The death throes of the chickens my grandfather made me kill when I was a kid lasted hours.'

The baby smiled. He'd heard his first joke. I'm not actually sure whether babies really can smile or whether they just move their gobs in a certain way that makes adults think they're grinning. If you ask me, you need to get over a few rotten experiences first before you can start laughing.

Dmitry had recovered from the shock and started pouring abuse on Martina. He hadn't raped her, after all, it wasn't his baby, and it would a pretty poor state of affairs if he, as an Albanian, had to take the blame for the filthy deeds of other Albanians. He might happen to be Albanian, that didn't make him Albania. They were the kind of things he said. And although he was right, I just wanted him to shut the hell up and murder that kid pronto. Now I was stuck with it.

It had started to cry in the meantime and that was the last thing we needed. Soon the whole corridor would be awake and the plan would degenerate into a complete fiasco. There was only one way out, and that was to put the kid on the breast. There was no choice, Martina had to realize that and grit her teeth, *she* had to get the baby to shut up. She had to calm the bloody thing down, because as much as we wanted to, it was beyond us.

She did it. Madonna with child. The Renaissance must have been a wonderful time.

Maqsood comforted Dmitry, who was sitting there with his head in a bucket, Martina breast-fed, Lidia stuck her head out the door to see whether it was all quiet in the corridor and saw that things were fine, I smoked the first cigarette in my life that I felt like I really needed. Finally it was quieter, calmer, and as long as that kid was drinking instead of crying, we could think about what to do. It seemed to us that Igor was the only one who could resolve the situation.

Me back to my room. Me shaking Igor with my heart in my mouth. Me explaining the situation to him. And begging him for his help.

Still groggy with sleep, Igor appeared beside Martina's bed. His massive body. The polar look in his eyes. Permafrost. The knuckles he cracked. He was our man. And when the baby had drifted off to sleep we lay the little bundle of flesh in his masses of muscle. Please let it be quick. Part of me was glad that Igor could take out his frustrations on an innocent baby, that he had a chance to vent some of his rage. It would calm him down, after tonight it would be a good bit easier for me to share a room with him.

He just stood there. The same mistake that I had made. The five minutes he stood there silently holding the baby turned into ten. We thought he was priming himself, gathering his strength. And those ten minutes became a quarter of an hour. The quarter of an hour became half an hour. No one said a word. No one dared to say a word, especially not to Igor. Then he lay the child down on its mother's body and said, 'Sorry.' I've never heard anyone say 'sorry' in a drier voice.

Martina had to do it herself. That was the only way it would make any sense. Only by doing it herself would she take revenge on her rapist in her own way. We agreed that it was better to leave her alone with the baby until she was finished. She could knock on our door. Maqsood had managed to smuggle in a couple of bottles of especially noxious booze and it was only logical that we should wait in his room. Igor, Dmitry, Maqsood, Lidia, the bottles and me. Take a slug and pass the bottle. Take a slug and pass the bottle.

Martina's timing was perfect, she knocked on the door just when the last bottle was almost drained.

It was Igor who went with her. He wrapped the child in a Sunday paper, like so many potato peels, and carried it to reception. Officially stillborn, strangled by the umbilical cord.

The child would have been called Bastard.

Naturalization Exercise No. 4545KFSD45b:
'Louis Paul Boon Tells a Gag at the Tavern'

sure you don't keep your ears in your pockets and like everyone else you're constantly hearing things, usually the kind of things you're not interested in anyway but that's another story, walking around the place and hearing all kinds of things you must have heard that darkies are supposed to have a longer dong. people wouldn't be people if they didn't make a mountain out of every molehill so you're hardly surprized to see them trying to turn a flute into an organ pipe now. and it's only because you happen now and then to take your mind off your troubles by kicking a ball around with the pub team you've been a member of going on fourteen years that you came into a position to get to the bottom of that story about the long doodle seeing as your team recently recruited a new player a negro who wants to have a wash after the game like everyone else. alone together men have no secrets unless they're doing it with each other's wives but otherwise there's not much that will embarrass them and definitely not their hairy arses. it's just that you don't have any say in it and everyone has to make do with the equipment he's born with; nothing to be ashamed of, nothing to be proud of, although it's the nature of science to never stand still and nowadays if you have the desire and the dough to go with it you can have them patch together the size dick you always dreamed of. and science, it goes on and on, but never in the direction that will let you implant the set of brains that will finally let you remember what's worth remembering. anyway, you're no doubting judas, or was it thomas, but still you prefer to see something with your own eyes before you believe what people say, so you keep your eye on the negro and jump half out of your skin when he comes up next to you in the showers. he was called so, so he was, and his tool, you have to admit it, it really was so long that you immediately fell back with astonishment. my god that wasn't human anymore, that was half an elephant, that's what you said to yourself, lode, that's something you'd better get to the bottom of sonny-jim, and you enquire of the fellow who is impressive both horizontally and vertically how he got himself a bazooka like that, whether that was the work of god above with a magnifying glass stuck on the end of his monocle during creation and you admit that you wouldn't say no to a couple of inches more yourself. men alone together you see. the artilleryman answers, hang a brick on peter's head until he's long enough. and there you have it, the demystification of the elongated dong in a nutshell, all you had to do was hang a brick on your dick and you'd stretch it. you had a few bricks lying around the stable, surplus from when you built your house with your own two hands, and it was a matter of minutes rather than hours before you'd tied that weight onto your middle leg thinking: length is suffering. you walked around like that for a week, a whole week of your wife wondering what's our lode doing with a cobblestone hung on his balls and you answering her, that's not a cobblestone, it's a brick, and it's not hung off my balls, it's hung off my dong, to make it longer. and then you saw a twinkle in her eyes that are still beautiful even now and was encouraged to tie on not one, but two bricks. and it helped. you can't expect everything at once. Rome was not built in a day either, but after three weeks, although your prick still had exactly the same dimensions, it had already turned completely black.

Jingle All the Way

I am probably a real Catholic because I pretended to be one and profited from it. To mark the occasion of Christmas, a festive dinner was held in the refectory, hallelujah, and since I have, in the past, held my head under a running tap now and then, it wasn't a barefaced lie when I told them I'd been baptized.

There was music. Christmas carols that they throw in free of charge on a CD when you buy a kilo of coffee at the supermarket, ghastly, but music all the same. The festive dinner consisted of hot chocolate and buns that a local baker had donated to the centre in a fit of Christian charity. The buns were good, I ate three because I couldn't get my hands on a fourth, and drained my mug of hot chocolate with fanatical religious devotion. ('Security is a way of life' is printed on those mugs in four languages, given to us by a company because of a manufacturing fault somewhere on the inside. I've got plenty of time to think about this sentence, about what it's supposed to mean, but I can't come up with a decent explanation. I can't get it off my mind, that sentence, that terrible sentence – security is a way of life – and I can't help but think of Lidia who was somewhere in a container around that time. Security is a way of life. Had her ship left yet?)

To our great joy and astonishment, the management came up with a crate of cider. If the Muslims had scored two crates of cider for one of their religious festivals, I would have had great difficulty in suppressing my proselytizing fervour.

Alcohol has the quality of robbing people of their true nature. I love alcohol. Two glasses were enough for the Africans as well and suddenly they started singing *Zan Vevede, Oh Holy Night*. The women swung their bums, two immense hemispheres, making the night really holy, the rest of the refectory clapped their hands. I could imagine similar scenes taking place in old people's homes at that same moment. There too, sitting between trays of sedatives, they covered their liver spots with paper hats and were full of the Lord. With each pill a little more.

Just that morning we had buried Sedi in a grave no one will ever visit. Next to him, Martina's unwanted child is dissolving in complete rottenness. White are the breakers at sea, white is the Christmas Lidia dreamed of. I miss her. And I miss my camera. In the meantime I've started trembling so badly that it's questionable whether I'll ever be able to take another photo without a tripod again. Whether I'll ever be able take another photo. Whether I'll ever be able.

Igor wasn't thinking of boxing on this peaceful day for all people of goodwill and escaped into music, and I wasn't the only one he stunned in the process. He stood up at the table, the centre of attention, lifted one arm up in the air and sang. *Na nebe stoyala yasnaya zvezda*. A star is twinkling in the sky. His voice was as deep as his misery, his throat a mineshaft, the sound bubbled up out of it like water from a blocked sewer. It churned like blood from a throat that's been cut, it dripped like filth from an intestine. Black is too hopeful a colour to give to this voice. A singer was the last thing I would have suspected in Igor. More Russians had started singing now, joining him. *Na nebe stoyala yasnaya zvezda*, and it was only natural for me to wonder whether Lidia was now wearing the knickers with the twinkling stars. She will write to me if she survives the crossing. She will wait for me if I have the balls to take ship on a palette of tiles. She will. She left with a sense of the future and without me.

She's sailing. The water rocks her. To England. She's got herself a breath of fresh air, she's seen a bit of the world.

Negatives

'Pretend I'm not even here,' the photographer says and I despise him.

There are two kinds of press photographers, Canonites and Nikonians, these two are irreconcilable and act like stubborn militants of their camera brand. He's got a Nikon hanging on his fat stomach, immediately making me doubt the man's knowledge of photography. What's more he works in black and white, B&W, the snobs would say, I can see the films bulging out of his pouch: Ilford XP2, 400 ISO. He has the pretensions, the lack of pretension of an artist who likes it grainy. The kind of yob who blathers on about David Hockney's brainwaves, I'd bet a carton of cigarettes on that, and when he feels like a glass of champagne or a bit of fluff in his bed, he blows up a few photos, hangs them on a gallery owner's wall and organizes an opening for the clique from the photo club Click.

Here at the asylum centre, people are glad to

have a photographer arrive. It's a change from the daily grind. The residents have finally got something to do besides hang around the radiators blowing smoke rings. Asia – with the arse you'd need a wide-angle lens for – showered this morning until she'd used up all the hot water, then jumped into her fanciest clothes. She'd do better to drop her pants, then her molested fanny would get in the papers and people would know why she's asking for asylum. Maybe that could stir up public opinion. That's what fannies are for, after all, to stir. I swear it, everyone around here has buffed up their mug and their shoes and what for? So they'll have a nice portrait on their grave. Even Anna has swapped her Adidas tracksuit for the outfit of a first holy communicant so that she won't look like the starvation-line whore she's always been and always will be. Vanity is the phenomenon that makes people proud of looking like someone they're not. I know all about it, I had enough of them in front of my lens, before.

Thanks to the container deaths in Ireland and Italy, every newspaper worth the name suddenly wants to do something about asylum seekers and this photographer gnat is the chosen one who's been dispatched with a few rolls of film to release a few stomach-turning pictures into the world. That's definitely his ambition, in his thoughts he's already winning the Golden Eye, the Silver Lens and the Bronze Tripod at the Delhi Belly Photo Festival. He can see his work circling the globe and hopes that Amnesty International will print his lucky shots on their stationery.

He's going to be one of the greats, he can already picture himself on a runway in a Catholic country somewhere in the tropics asking the pope, 'Johannes, mate, could you kiss the ground again 'cause I don't think I quite got it that time round.' And the pope really does drop down to the ground again to plant another smacker on the tarmac, the man's an apostle and he wants to get as many photos as possible so that God gets the best PR imaginable, and he kisses it again, and he kisses and he kisses, until his holy lips are covered with blisters as big as balloons. That's what the photographer is thinking, I can feel it, and, even more strongly, I can feel that he'd better not give me a hard time or I'll wring his bloody neck for him.

Surgeons are babies when they have to go on the table themselves, photographers die when a lens is aimed in their direction.

'*What is your name?*' asks Mr. Nikonian in English, obviously trying to play it along the lines of: let's keep it nice and friendly, I'll just take a few snaps, you'll feel a slight jab but it won't hurt a bit.

'Bipul Masli,' I tell him, 'but feel free to call me Bhopal Muesli. I speak Dutch by the way.'

My name doesn't mean a thing to him, the only photographer he's heard of walks around in *his* clothes, maybe that newspaper should get him to start drawing cartoons.

'You do indeed speak Dutch. And very well, by the sound of it.'

The slimeball.

'Just pretend I'm not here.'

What does the clown take me for? As far as I'm concerned he doesn't even exist, let alone that I'd pretend he's not there.

He checks the light and sets up his camera, meanwhile asking a number of semi-professional questions, presumably to put me at my ease.

'So where do you come from, Mr., uh, Masli?'

'From Carpetland. Born and bred.'

'If you like, you could sit by the window and stare out for a bit, that would be nice.'

Nice? Does this joker really think it's nice to stare out through a window? At the lawn, the clothesline, the pétanque court nobody plays on because it's too cold, the barbed wire. There must be a million photos of people staring out of windows, when Burt Glinn took a photo for *Magnum* of a meditative Sammy Davis Jr. looking out a window, he set off a craze, but this amateur doesn't know that. He doesn't know anything.

'Could you rest your head on your right hand?'

I don't move.

'Your right hand, sir... Do you understand?'

'Yes, yes, the right hand is the hand with the thumb on the left. Take your photo and piss off.'

'I realize it's not much fun, but I'm almost done.'

He's persistent, I've got to give him that, so I stare out of the window. Not to do him a favour, just to get him out of my room as soon as possible. And he waits and he waits before taking his photo. He hasn't taken a single shot. He sits there studying me and checking his composition in the viewfinder and I wonder whether he's planning to do anything at all when a fly comes and lands on my head, comes and shits on my head, and he finally clicks the shutter, thanks me and leaves.

Postscript

This book would probably have never been written if the Flemish magazine *Deus Ex Machina* had not asked me to write a piece about asylum seekers. To immerse myself in the subject, I spent several days at a reception centre for asylum seekers in Arendonk, and without that bath I would not have been able, qualified or entitled to start this book.

I was there in December 2001 and it was bitterly cold. The attack on the WTC towers in New York was still front page news, the articles all reflected the fear that the world order was about to tumble, and Muslims everywhere were scared that they were going to be held to blame. During my stay, some twenty people died at sea on container ships, and many more were waiting on the docks to increase that number. When I completed the first, rough version of the manuscript of this book, some seven months later, none of the many asylum seekers on whom I had modelled *Problemski Hotel* had received a positive decision. Some had returned to their countries voluntarily, a few had been sent back under duress, others had disappeared or gone underground. Most of them were still at the centre, waiting for a hearing or a letter.

To avoid misunderstandings, I feel obliged to state that I made up about half of these stories and that not one of the stories contains a lie.

Finally I would like to express my gratitude to and admiration for the entire staff of the Arendonk asylum centre Totem, I would like to thank the Flemish Literature Fund for their support for this project, and I dedicate this book to the now deported Maqsood and his hundreds of thousands of fellow sufferers.